Copyright

G000067719

All rig

The characters and eve
fictitious. Any similarity t   , living or dead, is
coincidental and not intended by the author.

No part of this book may be reproduced, or stored in a
retrieval system, or transmitted in any form or by any
means, electronic, mechanical, photocopying, recording,
or otherwise, without express written permission of the
publisher.

ISBN-13: 9798478466657

FINDING GRACE

Every parent's nightmare ...
but it begs the question. How
far would you go?

Day 1 - Wednesday

'Sam, come on, open the door ... please?'

Jed knocked, then again, calling out for Sam to let him in. To his right, another door slowly opened and he could see an eye peeping through. He raised his hand to apologise to the neighbour for the disturbance and waited for the door to close.

Lowering his voice, Jed pleaded once more for his colleague to open the door. Moments passed so Jed checked his phone to see if Sam had read any of his messages. Further along the hall another door opened and an elderly neighbour watched as Jed returned his phone to his pocket.

'She hasn't been out for days' she stated. Jed walked towards her but this caused her to step back, so he paused.

'It's ok' he reassured her *'I'm just checking on her, that's all. We work together'* and with that, he pulled out a small card and offered out his hand.

The old lady reached for it and then with her glasses balanced on the bridge of her nose, she raised her eyebrows and studied his name.

'Jed Brown' she muttered; Jed nodded.

'That's me'. He said and asked if she would be willing to call him if she had any concerns about his friend and to his surprise, she agreed.

'*You look for people then?*' she asked and once more looked at the card in her hand.

'*Yes, that's right*' he replied '*I've worked with Sam for years. She's on leave at the moment and I haven't heard back from her, so I was a little worried you see ...*' but before he could finish the sentence, the old lady smiled, displaying her broken brown teeth.

'*So, **she's** missing then?*' she chortled. Jed returned a wry smile but the old girl refused to miss out on the opportunity

'*Not such a great advert for a Missing Persons Bureau, eh?*' she sniped. '*If you can't find one of your own?*'

Now she stepped into the hall way and allowed the heavy door to rest against her.

'*She is in*' she said in a matter-of-fact way. Jed's eyes widened.

'*I keep an eye on things round here*' she replied smugly '*... and she hasn't been out for days. We're used to her coming and going all hours of the day and night so it's unusual. I guess you could say I would be good at your job ... you know, noticing stuff? They say it's the little things, don't they?*'

'*Well, if I'm ever in the business for a new partner, I will be sure to let you know*' Jed replied and with that he turned away, but not before writing a short note for Sam and slipping it under her door.

'*If you do see her*' he continued, '*please ask her to give me a call*?' The lady raised her hand in acknowledgement and allowed the heavy door to close behind her.

Jed placed his hand on Sam's door, drew breath and whispered.

'*You're not going through this alone*'

He waited for a second in the hope her neighbour was right but moments passed, so reluctantly he walked away.

But just as Jed got to the first staircase the door above opened and Sam leaned over the balcony.

'*Jed*' she called and with that he raced up the stairs, climbing two at a time, his arms wrapping around Sam and pulling her close.

'*I'm not dead Jed … not yet anyway*' Sam released herself from his grip and pushed back her apartment door, gesturing they go inside. Again, the door at the end of the hallway opened and the old lady once more appeared, her hand raised to Jed, still clasping his business card. '*Told you*' she said and this time, closed her door with finality.

'*Don't say that! You've had me worried*' he said but this time Sam didn't reply, she walked over to the kettle and sat two mugs down on the counter.

Jed looked around the apartment and it was evident that nothing much mattered to Sam at the moment, from taking care of herself personally, or her home. There was clutter all around but one wall of the apartment was neat, precise and organised. Jed walked over to the other end of the living room and studied the detailed timeline.

There were photographs, small handwritten notes, post its, string joining different dates, along with a catalogue of searches and information already taken and thoughts to come.

Jed sighed aloud and this caught Sam's attention.

'*What*' she snapped. '*I'm on an enforced break ... for the good of my health apparently?... and I'm just going to stop searching for my granddaughter?*' Sam slammed the coffee cup down in front of Jed causing a little to spill over.

'*Hey*' Jed bit. '*Not me Sam! I haven't stopped, nor will I ever stop searching. We're in this together, you know we are*'

He tried to touch Sam's arm as she brushed passed and watched as she returned to the kitchen to retrieve her cup. She stared straight ahead and tried desperately to keep her breathing controlled and her emotions in check, then slowly closed her eyes and whispered into her cup, loud enough for Jed to hear, that she was sorry for being sharp.

He moved a pile of books off one of the sofas nearest the fire and sat down, then pointed to the other and asked Sam to sit, just for a moment. Begrudgingly Sam walked to the sofa, pulled her dressing gown around her legs and sat opposite, her eyes red and sore; the lack of sleep had seriously taken its toll.

The apartment wasn't huge, two-bedroom apartments in this part of London were pretty pokey at the best of times but this one was rented due to the proximity of their office and knowing the times of day and night they would be working on a case, it just had to be close enough for Sam to get home, get a little shut eye and then back to the office the moment anything changed or when new information arrived.

There were two larger windows looking out to the street below and the 2nd floor gave a great view over the park, which also allowed for some much-needed light.

The open plan kitchen/living room area had a small breakfast bar but that was never used as breakfast was usually a coffee on the way to the office and even the bedrooms were rarely used. Sam had lost count of the times she collapsed on the sofa, only to wake, shower (*if time*) and go again.

She had divorced around 15 years ago and although amicable, her ex-husband blaming her work for their breakdown, she was also aware he had been seeing someone and, in a way, it helped her walk from the marriage with a clearer conscience. She used to ask him to put himself in her position, saying imagine if you were desperate to find a loved one or seeking justice but the Police had done all they could, evidence had run dry or if you knew that a case was closed and you still had questions? ... how on earth could she take time out to go for dinner, or to the cinema?

'*Seriously*' she would argue '*How can I switch off and enjoy myself when someone's child is missing and who knows what is happening to them? The time I am wasting socially means they could be further and further away. It just isn't possible to have a normal home life*' and that was the truth of the matter. That conversation was a familiar one, yet the only thing he used to repeat at the end of her pouring out her frustration and upset was '*wasting time*?'

So, there was an easier life for him out there and she wished him luck.

For Sam, well, she was on the never-ending merry-go-round and there was no getting off until everyone was saved or found; that's how it felt to her and everyday someone else would be knocking on the door, begging for help; what chance did she have?

Now in her early 50s, her work felt like a map of her life. Every success in finding someone missing was a milestone. She could place those years as momentous ones, but sadly, there were also year's best forgotten.

'*Garden leave*' Sam muttered, then wiped a

tear from her eye. '*It feels like I'm losing her*' she said. Jed placed down his coffee and leaning forward, rested his elbows on his knees and gestured with his hands for Sam to stop.

'*We're far from losing her*' he whispered.

'*Bloody garden leave!*' she repeated. '*If I worked in a shop, well then, ok*' she went on

'*I wouldn't be interested in the welfare of the shop or the staff; in fact, if I was not doing the best I could for them, fair enough, send me home, but in our line of business you are literally stopping me from using resources to save a life! I'm going mad!*'

Jed passed a tissue and waited while Sam wiped her eyes and blew her nose.

'*Ok, listen*' he said. '*You have me, the team are also working hard but the first thing you must do, is not lose your shit!*' he said sharply. Sam continued wiping her face but looked up as he spoke firmly.

'*Grace has been missing for 5 months now?*' he stated, his brow quizzical, Sam corrected him straight away.

'*6 months Jed, nearly 6 months! That's a huge amount of time*'

Jed's eyes widened as he knew all too well the chances of finding a child gets harder as time passes.

'*We are in the best position to help her and look*

at it like this' he continued. '*At work you had a duty of care for **all** cases, not just your own, I get that*?' Sam agreed.

'*Now you have all the time you need to focus on what's best for Grace and what we need to do for her and I am telling you, we can give her more time than you realise because you will be able to let me know any developments and I can look into them, officially, where you can't and I can check databases that are still live?*' Sam nodded, acknowledging as Jed continued. '*Every day the team are checking and cross checking. We all want to be the one who gets the break, okay?*'

'*Okay?*' he repeated, his voice now taking up strength and momentum. '*Look, we are a Missing Persons Unit with power behind us ... money is not an issue and resources are easier for us to attain, we have the support from Police in the UK and Internationally and I don't just mean through my old contacts either*' Jed used his hands to communicate reassurance.

'*Sam, I'm telling you what you already know, but please hear me? We have so many contacts across the board, you know we do and of course you feel shut out at the moment, but you are not seeing this for the opportunity that it presents*' He reached forward and placed his hand on Sam's, causing her to look up and for a moment offer a fleeting smile.

Sam adjusted her posture, finding encouragement in his words.

She had felt terribly torn knowing that cases she had been working on became second place next to looking for Grace; even knowing the Police were heavily involved and doing what they could, it was never enough.

To be fair to the Agency, they allowed her to stay on longer than perhaps they should, hoping she would be able to continue doing what she did best and words to that effect had been discussed when news of Grace's abduction had first come to light.

Sam promised her superiors that if they allowed her to search in her own time, double checking information and talking to the Police within her capacity as an Agent; using the resources available, she would continue to focus on all cases, while the Police continued in their search. But the reality became very clear only a few months in when Sam's outbursts forced the Agency Chief to give her a warning, followed by another and eventually leave was suggested before she destroyed any hope of returning.

Sam had one daughter, Mia, 36, now married and living about half an hour away. They had always been close and yes, though she had to accept that her ex-husband did most of the parenting, Sam made sure any time she spent with Mia outside of work, was fun and Mia had always assured Sam that she hadn't felt left out, or unloved.

In fact, she had praised her Mother on a few occasions for being strong and independent, especially when she herself went on to further her own career and open a graphic design company; leaving her with little choice but to employ a Nanny to help with Grace.

She also said she could appreciate how her own Father had been amazing, working his shifts around her but unfortunately times had changed and Grace's Father Joe had to work long hours and struggled to keep on side with his boss; a few times Mia told him to jack it in, suggesting Joe help with Grace and they let the Nanny go, but it was obvious Joe did not see that as part of his role.

Mia felt they could manage financially even though her company had only been up and running a couple of years but Joe was of the mind that it was the man's place to support the family and struggled to accept his wife as the breadwinner.

It caused many disagreements and Joe had even caused an argument one Christmas at the dinner table after a few too many drinks, telling Sam that if Mia had learnt how to be a mother from her example, Gracie would not be spending time with so many Nannies! That hurt Sam terribly but sadly no one came to her defence and the apology offered by Mia to the quietened faces around the table was in regard to excess alcohol, as opposed to the personal attack on her.

Now however, there was a grievance and perhaps

not even realised fully by the two women. Mia had turned to her Mother the moment Grace's absence was known and when your Mother is a senior figure at a Missing Persons Agency, you understandably feel this puts you ahead of the game.

But as the days, weeks and months passed, communication between the family was fraught, bitter even, wrapped up in pain and disappointment that you can't rely on your nearest and dearest at this most crucial time in your life. The silence between them was deafening.

Grace was a delight and at the time of going missing she had just turned 2. Her blonde curls sat around her rosy cheeks, her chubby little hands touching everything she could reach and her big blue eyes full of question; so inquisitive.

Sam thought of her every day, praying for news, praying she was safe and not harmed. Most parents have had those nightmares, waking up in a sweat, panicking their child was lost, or that they couldn't save them from a terrible situation, only to find within a few seconds of opening their eyes, they were safely asleep in their bed.

Sam didn't sleep for a long period of time and she was certain her daughter Mia couldn't either. Mia went back to work a couple of months after Grace went missing as some of her employees called to say they were being chased by companies who were waiting for their designs to be finalised and money owed was being blocked, threatening them as a whole.

Mia would walk into the office, only for voices to fall silent, reassuring smiles or nods from staff and occasionally someone bravely asking if there was any news. She did what she had to do, then returned home, working as much as she could away from the pitying expressions.

Only 36 and married to Joe for just a handful of years before Grace came along and with her business taking off, perhaps timing wasn't the best but Mia wanted it all, something she had in common with Sam.

Text messages between Sam and Mia were easier and they were the most frequent way to keep in touch. Hearing each other's voices had provoked tears and/or harsh unforgiving words and that didn't help either.

Sam had also been guilty of not answering her phone when she saw Mia's name on the screen. She knew the emotional fall out could cause her to step back or be off her game which couldn't continue in the office.

Jed rose from the sofa and walked over to the timeline.

'This is incredible' he said as Sam joined him, then pointing at a photograph Jed inquired about the man pictured.

'*He may not be anybody*' Sam told him. '*It's one of those things though, I can't place him with the van? You know that would ring alarm bells with us but I have tried Jed and he's a ghost?*'. Jed glanced towards Sam, then back at the picture.

'*Where did you get it?*' he asked. '*Did you take it?*'

Sam shook her head. '*No, it was Frosty*' she said, waiting for his reaction.

'*Frosty?!!*' Jed demanded and immediately Sam placed her hand on his arm.

'*Don't start Jed, I will use whoever I have to, it's just another perspective ok*'

Jed strode away from the wall and looked out the window and down to the park, drawing in deep breaths and trying to compose himself.

'*He should be hung*' he growled. Sam joined his side once more and this time they stood shoulder to shoulder.

It was picturesque below, dog walkers passing by, families having a picnic, a ball being kicked about by a group of children and parents walking along the path with pushchairs and small children alongside with scooters.

'*A peaceful scene*' Sam had once remarked when she first came to view the apartment, now she tried not to look as the reality of everyday life was too painful.

Sam looked to Jed, knowing how he felt about Frosty. She would never have asked him for anything if convicted, but it's like they say, unless you're in that position, you don't know what you would do.

'It's like doing a deal with the devil' he said, as he acknowledged Sam glaring at him.

'And I would make that deal over and over again' she said. *'I would give my life willingly, whatever it takes and I will use the scum of the earth to help me find Gracie and then I would thank them from the bottom of my heart … you know how desperate I am?'*

Jed closed his eyes and slowly exhaled. He heard her words, he knew what Sam had been dealing with these past 5 months and although he had seen things during his career that would stay with him for the rest of his life, he could never truly understand the desperation or despair that she was going through.

Jed was married to Lisa, they had been together for over 16 years and were now the proud parents of twin boys, aged 5. When Grace had first been reported missing Jed admitted that he went home in the middle of the night and woke them, just to hold them. His wife had gotten out of bed and the couple headed downstairs to talk privately where she held him and asked him how long he could continue to work at a place that only ever brought him pain and despair?

He asked her if she would want him to be the one to find their boys, if they were missing? Lisa agreed, of course she would, he was the sort of man who, if said would do something, would do it, so yes, he was the one she would want to find them.

'*Well, I have to be that man for Sam*' he continued and they held each other whilst he explained Grace had been taken. Lisa sobbed and, on that night, Jed wept with her.

Jed's colourful past had brought him full circle. He spent most of his adult career with the Police Force, choosing to be particularly guarded when conversation raised its head. After meeting Lisa, he knew he would have to reconsider his options and the need for change. It confused her at the time, but he asked her to trust him and said it wasn't a life for a family.

The Agency was an enticing safe haven and when he accepted an internal transfer to London, the Missing Persons Agency had been running on the floor below for a number of years. He had offered great advice to the team over time and they clicked with him instantly and eventually he accepted the chance to join them.

'*An Agency with a difference*' that's how it was sold to him, where his '*skills could be utilised and experience harnessed*'. Jed suggested a bumper sticker?

But that was it. Jed handed in his notice and headed to the floor below to start a new career. He had the best of both, his experience within the Police, connections and contacts available to them all, better hours and pay!

Frosty had been involved in one of Jed's first cases when he transferred with the Police. They had been looking for a 15-year-old boy for over 48 hours. His parents said he had given them a bit of attitude of late, although his dad felt he was just *'finding his feet'* and that his age group was a lot about peer pressure; his mum however, was desperately worried.

She said he used to talk to her when his dad wasn't around, telling her he felt scared by boys in the neighbourhood. A couple went to his school and they followed him home and bullied him and the bravado was just for his dad's sake; she knew he was struggling.

She begged him to let her talk to someone, let her pick him up from school but he wouldn't allow it, saying he would get a harder time if they saw him getting into his mum's car.

Now he was missing and she had defied all the guidance, including that of her husband who had asked her to give the boy some breathing space, she knew this was not the norm, this was out of character and whether he liked it or not, she was going to find their son.

The second day of absence, having exhausted all other contacts in the local neighbourhood, his dad started to see they may have a problem and took it upon himself to call on friends and family to help with a search.

They made the local news and when the Agency got involved, they had even more media coverage, including a spokes person who asked for everyone to search outhouses, sheds, or places that could be used for refuge.

Sam at that time had a few cases she was working on with her team and Jed was heading up a smaller unit with the Police, when he was alerted to the disappearance of Max.

Sadly, there are too many predators to watch and even more frightening is the fact that statistically most young people are in danger from their own family or close relatives, than outsiders.

Jed had spent a lot of time with Max's Father and Uncles and even some of their closest friends and this had been so frustrating and time wasting for them, but Jed continued to investigate, leaving nothing unturned.

It was only 4 days into Max's disappearance that Jed received a call from a contact to say they may have information on a missing 15-year-old boy and Jed headed off to meet him. That's where he first met 'Frosty'.

Geoff Frost had been in trouble with the Police all his life and had been a self-confessed watcher of children but had managed to keep his feelings under control. He said he would like to help and by using information and in turn by being proactive, he felt he had more control over his own behaviour and could manage his weakness. For a few years, there was no doubt, his help proved invaluable.

Jed never held back his disdain for Frosty; in fact, Frosty threatened to quit helping on a number of occasions because of the way Jed berated him. He couldn't help how he felt, but he hadn't acted on it and didn't want to be that person. He accused Jed of being unprofessional, of being a hypocrite, saying he was good enough when it suited him, where a lead saved the day, but other than that? Frosty was a lowlife.

Jed spent hours with Frosty and together they replayed time, placed Max in certain streets, a car, identified faces and so on and eventually Jed had enough to call for support and they entered a house where Max was found.

He had been beaten, left in a downstairs basement with his ankle chained to a radiator and a half-filled bottle of water lay nearby, but just out of reach.

Frosty had always left the scene before a break in and Jed had been more than happy for him to go. It was also agreed that if he was to continue being a source then undercover was the safest, allowing him to mix in circles; it made sense that he was not linked with the Unit.

It was years later that Jed found out the real truth about Frosty and that he hadn't managed to keep his hands to himself as he proclaimed. He had been caught with a few photographs and busted, then further incriminating material was found and although they couldn't link him with abductions, he was in receipt of material, linking him to a network.

He offered to help Investigators as part of a Court settlement and to keep him out of prison he became a narc, so he was well known to the Police.

His own wife had taken their daughter and moved away when she became suspicious about his behaviour and her daughter's reaction towards him. It confirmed their fears but nothing was proven.

Jed however, was not about to let him have one second more of his time, even if it meant him losing his job. Thankfully the Police Unit believed in Jed and where they could support him, they would, so Frosty and Jed no longer worked together.

Sam contacted Frosty directly. She had been in touch with him a few months ago and asked him to do some digging for her.

In the past when the Police were supporting the Agency on a case, Frosty was called upon to provide information, but always supported by a member of the Force.

Frosty knew about her granddaughter's abduction and told her he had seen it on the local news but Sam believed that may not be the case.

She reminded him that she had always dealt with him respectfully and until something concrete came along to incriminate him, she wanted to believe in his wish to better himself and this was another opportunity to show her faith in him was well placed.

Frosty told her there was talk of a cleaning company moving drugs around the City in vans and the photograph of the man with the van was someone to watch. He sent her the picture and said he would get back to her with more information.

'*Drugs*?' Jed repeated.

'*I know, random maybe, but while he is looking at him it may have some bearing on something else*' Sam walked back to the wall and tapped on a picture further up.

'*See him*' she said, tapping again on the face of a bearded man. '*He was seen talking to our ghost with the van and we can place him outside the laundromat, off Grosvenor; near the gentlemen's club …*' Sam waited for Jed to acknowledge, then join her.

'*Ok*' said Jed, his voice trailing.

'*Well,*' continued Sam '*This guy is the brother*

of Sir Geoffrey and if ever there was a dodgy bastard, it's him!' she finished.

Jed leaned in to study the picture closely and could see a bearded man in his 40s, carrying a suit and a briefcase and on closer inspection noticed the chains around his neck.

'He hardly looks like the brother of a toff' he added.

Sam agreed, strange as it was, but she knew his older brother Sir Geoffrey and had come across him in the past. One of those families who appear untouchable, where money and power protect them but the sheer fact that Frosty was connecting our ghost with a van moving drugs around the City, contact with our bearded man, who in turn has opportunity of a vast clientele of rich business men; it would be a mistake at this stage not to add it to her timeline, yet it held no personal interest in her search for Grace that she could see, not yet anyway.

Jed moved to the left and looked closer to the day in question. A photograph of little Grace, smiling and clutching her blue bunny was pinned to a note above, with the date and time she was last known to be safe.

He lowered his eyes briefly and took in a short breath when Sam moved in closer and held his arm tightly. She lay her head against his shoulder and Jed took her hand and held it to his chest.

'*She has to be alive Jed; she just has to be …*' Sam's voice trailed off as she slowly cried.

Jed tapped her hand and tried to hold back his own tears, swallowing hard but managing a low mumble, saying she would be.

Sam rose her head and walked away.

'*But we both know the ugly truth*' she stated. Jed turned '*What chance does a child have? We've said ourselves in the past, that sometimes it would be better for a child not to survive?*'

Jed raised his voice. '*This isn't helping*'. He caught up with Sam who was now moving toward the other end of the room, making herself busy loading the dishwasher.

'*Why?*' she said, glaring at him. '*Because it's us, it's different?*' Jed again tried to keep the conversation positive but knew all too well it was a belief they had often shared during previous investigations.

'*She's so young Sam. There's a chance it's an abduction, ransom or possibly a family who are desperate for a child?*' Jed continued, his arms waving around as he tried to animate his frustration.

'*It's not a ransom Jed. No-one ever came forward for money and it's nearly 6 months later?*' She threw down a tee towel in frustration. '*It's more sinister, I just know it. The not knowing is the worst and I have made every possible evil scenario come to life in my mind and I only know one way to block it out and believe me, I have been close!'* Sam placed her head in her hands and broke down. Jed held her once again and for a moment no words were spoken.

'*Ok*' Jed finally broke the silence. '*Humour me and let's walk through it, from day 1.*' Jed walked her back to the wall; his arms spread out as he got closer '*There's a reason we call it the crazy wall*' he uttered.

Sam sighed '*Is it because it's all kinds of crazy?*' she smiled. It was an encouraging smile, however brief and Sam smacked him on the arm, then smiled again.

'*Thank you*' she murmured.

Sam pushed her dressing gown sleeves up to her elbows and stepped to the left-hand side of the wall.

'*What's that?*' asked Jed. Sam pointed high on the board and pointed to a question mark.

'*This?*' she asked. Jed nodded and Sam explained that it stood for the actual time Grace was last seen.

'*I thought we knew that, so why a question mark?*' he repeated. '*We know that on the afternoon she was with the Nanny, they returned from the park at 4.20pm?*' he stepped closer and pointed to a post-it underneath, before adding. '*There, we marked their arrival home at 4.20pm'*

Sam glanced at him, then lifted the note to see another, much smaller sticker, asking what had happened in that crucial 20 minutes from the Nanny being able to confirm she was with Grace, then realising she had gone?

'*They came here don't forget'* Sam spoke louder, with frustration.

'*Yeah, yeah, I know that'* Jed snapped. '*Sam, I just need to re-think this in my own head ok. Just walk me through it and who knows, something may click, stand out, it has to be worth it doesn't it?*' Jed turned to look Sam directly in the eyes as he made his statement, she paused to think about her reaction, then said once again that she was struggling to deal with time wasted and hadn't meant to shut him down. She really did need a second opinion, a second view point and trusted no-one else, like she did him.

'*Ok'* Jed faced the wall again. '*So, you were going to take over from the Nanny around 6pm, yeah?*' Sam agreed. '*But around 4.20pm, give or take a few minutes, the Nanny realised Grace was not in the living room and the door was ajar? Correct so far?*' Sam started to pace, nodding regularly and confirming when prompted.

'*I got the call'* she added, once more closing her eyes for a second as she tried to block out the painful reminder.

'*Sam, stay with me*' Jed pleaded. '*Yeah, you got the call and of course you headed straight home?*'

'*Yes, straight away*' Sam confirmed.

'*So, you had a record of 4.20pm on your phone from the call?*' Jed waited for the acknowledgement and when Sam replied yes, he carried on.

'*Ok, so the 4 – 4.20pm is our crucial window – too short for very much to happen you would think, but somehow no-one noticed anything unusual?*'

Sam looked back at Jed and returned to the wall.

'*We talked to everyone on the landing, you know how thorough we all were; the Police agreed neighbours were either out or inside their apartments and nothing unusual was noted*'

'*Now*' said Jed and he too started to take slow steps across the room, his hands in front of his face, occasionally clasped together in thought.

'*Obviously the Nanny was beside herself, but you feel there was nothing odd there?*' he looked for acknowledgement but Sam momentarily raised her eyes and flashed him a glare.

'*Everything Sam, everything has to be thought of, you know that ... come on*' Jed returned to his standing position in front of the wall.

'*She has been with Grace for 2 years and completely checked out so no, there was nothing untoward going on*' Sam spoke from the heart. '*She is a friend of the family and they have plenty of money before you mention that again, so there is no reason whatsoever for Grace to be in any danger whilst in her care, none!'*

'But she went missing whilst in her care; that's all I'm saying?'

Banging outside the apartment, in the hallway, brought their conversation to a halt and Jed pushed past Sam to get to the door.

When he looked outside, he could see a young man thumping on the door further down the hallway and called out to him.

'You ok buddy?

'I ain't your buddy' came the curt reply, so Jed stepped out, into the hallway.

'You live there?' he tried again.

'Yes, I live here and I don't need any assistance!' the sandy haired man thumped on the door again.

'Jose, unlock the door! You're causing a disturbance out here' Jed walked a few feet towards him.

'Actually, it's you causing a disturbance ...' he said with authority.

The man turned to face Jed square on and with a low growl to his voice he puffed out his chest and fronted him.

'You bored?' he asked. Jed stopped walking

and held out his hands.

'Not bored, just trying to get on with some work inside, that's all'

Jed placed his hands in his pockets and stood casually about 8 feet away from the disgruntled man. He shrugged his shoulders and offered to call the Police if the guy didn't desist in causing a disturbance but this just aggravated the situation further and with that the man rushed forward and knocked Jed's shoulder as he barged by, making his way back down the staircase, uttering expletives on the way.

Sam popped her head out and made a small whistle sound to Jed who was still watching the angry man leave the building, the huge wooden foyer doors below creaking as they squeezed together.

'Was he checked out?' he asked, as he made his way back to Sam's door.

'And who's Jose?' Jed closed the door behind them and pointed back.

'Are they new?' he asked.

'No, they've been here awhile according to Sally' Sam gestured to the opposite direction and Jed realised Sam was referring to the old lady he met that morning.

'Oh, she said she kept an eye on things around here' he paused for a moment and then could not help adding.

'*Pity she didn't see what was going on the day Grace was snatched eh?*' Sam stared back at him.

'*Not helpful*' she remarked.

Sam passed a cup of tea to Jed and for a moment a bit of normality filled the room. She found herself picking up a few clothes from the sofa and taking them to the bedroom where she threw them onto the bed and returned to move papers that were scattered on the coffee table, along with a pizza box and empty glasses that she returned to the kitchen.

'*Right ... so ...*' Jed continued.

'*How did they get in?*' he asked as Sam sipped her tea and placed herself once more by his side.

'*That is the question*' Sam sighed.

'*Blame was laid at Sylvia's side*' she looked puzzled and frustrated as she said it aloud.

'*Sylvia being the Nanny?*' Jed confirmed.

'*Yes, Sylvia being the Nanny*' Sam repeated, her tone a little sarcastic.

'*Odd though, wouldn't you say?*' Jed returned once again with his opinions of the Nanny.

'*Jed, I honestly don't believe she had anything to do with this and if you don't think I have checked and double checked, then you don't know me at all*'

Sam walked away and slumped down on the sofa.

'*No, don't sit down*' Jed barked.

'*Get back here, come on, we need to iron out the smallest detail; you know the drill Sam. Get up!*'

With that Sam hauled herself up once more and pulled her dressing gown off completely, standing in her leggings and long-sleeved pyjama top; she pushed her hair off her face and sighed loudly.

'*Ok, so no ... I do not believe Sylvia left the front door open; I do not believe Grace walked out into the hallway and obviously if she did, she was only 2, where the heck did she go?*' Sam splayed out her hands.

'*She didn't know how to use the lift; she couldn't do the staircase on her own and she sure as hell could not have opened or got out of those huge front doors!*'

Jed mumbled in agreement.

'*Fair enough*' he said.

'*So, someone took her. Someone took her from the apartment or from the hallway ... bear with me*' he interrupted his flow and raised his finger in the air.

'*If Sylvia had accidentally left the door ajar and Grace had walked out ...?*' Sam drew in a deep breath and finally agreed a yes, if that was the only two options they were left with.

'*Who else had a key?*' he asked and Sam raised

her eyes in thought.

'*Well, Mia of course and the Nanny … oh and me*' Sam continued '*All for the ease of covering Grace, but that's it. No neighbours or friends or even a spare, just us 3!*'

Jed thought again, then took Sam's hand in his.

'*Sam, there is no other answer, come on*' he implored.

'*If there was no break in, Grace was last seen around 4, you were at work, Mia was at work and the only one left with a key and had perfect opportunity was Sylvia?!*' he watched as Sam walked away defeated.

'*I know what you're saying, I hear you*' she said, exhaustion taking its toll. '*But don't you think if Sylvia was behind this, I mean if she needed Grace to go missing, it would have been better at the park? Somewhere where anyone could have taken her? Not making the move back here, leaving herself as the only possible suspect?*'

Sam's arms were spread and her face showing the same expression as Jed had seen many times over the years, the sheer audacity of a thought, the words that just didn't make sense and the frustration that someone is wasting air time by even thinking such a thing.

What Jed did know and what experience had shown them both was that it's often right in front of you, something that springs to your defence, that eventually allows itself to be seen and it had been there all the time. It was this type of frustration that usually showed itself to be true, if you just gave it the time it deserved.

'*Where is Sylvia now*?' Jed asked, his voice a little less abrasive now he had made Sam take stock of the facts.

'*No Jed, her parents have forbidden any contact at the moment. She has been in therapy for Christ's sake. She's only 20, can you imagine how devasting this must have been for her?*'

Jed sat down and let himself fall back into the sofa with a sigh of frustration.

'*I don't care Sam*' he whispered. '*I just want to explore everything, all over again and I know you do too, this isn't the time to consider anyone's feelings. We need to find Grace and you said earlier you would do whatever it takes?*' Jed waited for Sam to stop staring at him.

'*Get dressed*' he ordered, his voice a little more authoritarian this time and without question Sam rose and headed for the bedroom.

Jed leapt up and grabbed his jacket. '*I'll meet you outside*' he shouted. '*Just gonna check on that Jose woman*'

Jed walked a few doors along and tapped on Jose's door, not too loud, but hopefully loud enough for the tenant to hear. Very quickly he was aware there was someone home but the door did not open so he tapped again and this time spoke softly saying he was visiting his friend a couple of doors along and just wanted to check she was ok, having seen her partner leave earlier.

The door opened slightly and a chain held it close enough for Jose to look through.

'I'm fine, thank you' she said quickly, her eyes darting past him, taking a brief moment to see if anyone else was around.

'You sure?' Jed asked again.

Jose nodded, her sweaty brow caused her hairline to be damp and stuck to part of her forehead. Her reddened eyes were possibly due to a substance and there was certainly a smell seeping through the gap.

Jed nodded. *'ok then'* he said and with a little acknowledgement from Jose, the door closed and a lock turned on the other side.

'Strange' he thought as he returned to meet Sam fully dressed, coat in hand and hair swept up, ready to go.

'She ok?' Sam asked.

'That's a matter of opinion' he replied, his eye squinting and the corner of his mouth turned up *'very strange'*

On the drive to Sylvia's parents house, Sam took a moment to thank Jed again for showing up *'You left me no choice'* he laughed. *'Answer your friggin' phone woman!'*. Sam returned a slight smile and placed her hand on Jed's as he changed gear.

'Thank you anyway' she whispered.

Pulling into the drive at Sylvia's house, there was confirmation indeed that money was not an issue.

The large palatial manor house sat in its own grounds, adorned with trees and large flowering bushes either side of a gravel driveway.

The front door itself was the size of a small bathroom in width and as they rung the bell and waited, they could hear the echo of sound reverberating in the hallway. Seconds later Sylvia's Mother opened the door.

Her expression was not welcoming. In fact, she was pretty vocal from the moment they locked eyes, with Sam apologising before she had a chance to explain their presence.

'You promised Samantha!' barked Cynthia and she waved a housekeeper away, choosing to deal with her unwelcomed visitors herself.

Cynthia was in her early 50s and very well to do. She could have featured on the front of a 1950s housewife magazine, hair in waves, red lips and a figure to match the era.

'Forgive me Cynthia' Sam tried to say *'I know*

Sylvia is not to blame' but before she managed anything further Cynthia raised her voice again.

'Just leave!' she demanded and Sam reached out to touch her hand, begging her to just listen to them, for a moment.

Cynthia withdrew her hand and started to close the door but Jed stuck his boot inside and the door jolted, with a thud.

'Wait!' barked Jed. Cynthia looked down at his foot, then at Sam, ignoring Jed's request completely.

'Samantha!' she blasted.

Jed removed his foot and placed his hand on the heavy door to stop it closing further; stepping forward and making sure he was in Cynthia's eye line.

'Good morning' he grinned.

'Samantha was just about to explain our visit so if you would kindly allow her to do so?' he tilted his head to the side, inviting Sam to speak.

Sam gave Jed a sly glance, then told Cynthia that she realised the upset their visit would cause but she also knew that Cynthia would appreciate the importance of finding Grace, including bringing this ordeal to a close for Sylvia?

Cynthia glared at Jed then reluctantly opened the door and stood aside.

'Make your way to the drawing room' she in-

structed.

'*Thank you*' whispered Sam and with a little push of Jed, made their way to the room, as instructed.

'*See, money is not a motive*' she told him.

'*Sam, you know better than most that people with family money often rebel as they don't feel they have the right to independence or mummy and daddy don't understand them ... for pity's sake, why am I telling you what you already know*?'

Jed turned to face Sam. '*We are here to find Grace, stop pussy footing around this family!*'

They were still locked in a stare when Sylvia and her Mother entered the room. Sylvia looked as shaken today as she had done, nearly 6 months previous.

Sam begged her to not worry and invited her to sit down while they asked a few questions, but first she introduced Jed to them both.

'*I thought you were on leave*?' Sylvia asked, her voice trembling. Sam nodded and looked between the two women as she spoke.

'*Yes, still on leave but it's nearly 6 months now and we're no closer to finding Grace*' she told them. Sylvia pulled a tissue from her sleeve and started to sniffle; her Mother placed her arm around her shoulder in comfort.

'*I know it's tough Sylvia*' soothed Sam '*but my partner Jed may just spot something new, something we didn't talk about before so please, I am asking you from the bottom of my heart to allow us to talk over the events of that day, just 10 minutes?*' Sylvia nodded, unable to respond.

Sam sat down to be closer to Sylvia, but Jed stood by the fireplace.

'*Jed wasn't on this case at the time but he has been by my side and helping me as much as he can*'. Sylvia looked at Jed who smiled reassuringly and then spoke in a much gentler tone.

'*Hi Sylvia. Thank you for this. So, if I have it right, you came back from the park with Grace and you know she was with you around 4pm?*' he waited for her to acknowledge, then continued. '*Great, but may I ask how you know it was close to 4?*'

Sylvia stopped wiping her eyes and blew her nose gently.

'*We always tried to get back to watch Peppa Pig at 4 and it was the same that day*' she paused, her mind thinking back.

'*I use that time to make her tea, you know, while she's watching tv*' she looked to her Mother, then Sam, hoping they would understand; the sense it made to have a 2-year-old entertained while she cooked.

Sam agreed but it was pretty obvious Cynthia had

never had to worry about preoccupying a 2-year-old or the joy of Peppa!

'*What happened?*' Jed asked. '*Talk me through it please*?' he went on. '*Do you remember making her tea? What was it? With the layout of Sam's apartment, you would have been able to see her sitting on the sofa whilst you were making it, surely?*'

Cynthia raised her hand. '*... let her answer*' she snapped.

'*Apologies*' Jed waited, before adding '*In your own words and time but Sylvia please do something for me? Do not try to remember the situation or words you gave in your statement, if possible. Stop and think back to the day and walk me through it, as you remember it now. It really helps to think of a situation from a different view point and time can be a gift like that?*'

Sylvia tried to think and then with a burst of energy she started to relay events.

'*So, we headed home ...*' she paused while gathering her thoughts. '*I let her climb the stairs as it helped tire her out and I know that after her tea it would be bath and bed, so it helps*'

She sat up a little further and her Mother released her hand from her shoulders as she continued.

'*She kept saying 'Peppa' when we went in and that was because I used to mention it at the park, to get her to stop playing and get her to leave*' Sam smiled as she herself had bribed her that way and it was comforting to hear Grace being coaxed in a similar vain.

'*So up we went, step by step, 'Peppa' she kept saying and I was repeating it, yes Peppa ... up we go and then we were at the top'.* She stopped for a moment and then closed her eyes.

'*Take your time'* insisted Jed.

Sylvia began to panic. '*I, I can't ...'* Sam quickly touched her hand to calm her, saying she knew this was awful to think about, but it helped and if helping find Grace was what she wanted, then this was her way of helping.

Sylvia nodded and looking into Sam's eyes she continued.

'*I opened the door and put the pushchair inside'* she said.

'*Where was Grace then?'* asked Sam.

'*With me'* came the curious reply.

'*Yes, but was she ahead of the pushchair going in, or behind?'* asked Jed.

'*I don't understand?'* Sylvia said and Cynthia couldn't help but remind them all that Grace didn't go missing in the hallway, but whilst inside the apartment?

'*I know what I am asking'* Jed replied. '*Please, Sylvia, try and remember?'*

Sylvia again closed her eyes and then with a surprised voice blurted out.

'*Behind, yes, definitely behind because Sally had been waving to her … '*. Sylvia looked thrilled that she had remembered Grace's position when entering the apartment and waited for their reaction but the praise was not forthcoming.

Sam looked puzzled and flashed a glance at Jed who, within a few moments of talking with the star witness, had managed to highlight a small, maybe insignificant fact that Sally HAD been home that day … 'physic Sally' who kept an eye out and knew what was going on '*all the details*' she had boasted, '*the little things*' she had said.

Without expressing their thoughts to Sylvia, Jed swiftly gestured to continue.

'*We went inside and Grace was still asking for Peppa so I took her coat and shoes off and popped her on the sofa, turned on the tv and then went to the kitchen … that's it*' she said. Her hands now fidgeting on her lap.

Sam smiled reassuringly at Sylvia. '*Excellent, thank you for that*' she said kindly.

Jed placed his hands in his pockets and strode around the room, finally stopping and asking Sylvia to finish her recollection.

Sylvia whimpered a little and again withdrew her tissue.

'Okay' Jed asked quietly. '*Let's just get this over with*' he said. '*You cannot have been in the room with her the whole time or you would have seen her leave? Do you remember closing the door?*' he asked abruptly.

Sylvia snapped a defiant 'yes' and again Sam placed her hand over hers.

'*But you said Grace came into the room behind the pushchair?*' Jed reminded her, to which she nodded.

'*So, you would have been pushing the pushchair which meant you had entered the room before Grace?*' he widened his eyes, they were questioning enough for her to answer.

'*Yes, but as I said, she did enter the apartment as I took off her shoes and coat and put her on the sofa!*' Sylvia looked at their faces and then back to Sam. '*I put her on the sofa so she definitely came in with me Sam*'

Sam looked to Jed, unaware of where he was going with this but happy that he was taking so much time with the detail, anything new to grasp, was a start.

'*I'm asking because I'm wondering whether you put the pushchair down, went back and actually closed the door behind you OR did you put the pushchair down, pick up Grace and take her to the sofa, shoes and coat off and tv on before walking to the kit-*

41

chen and starting tea, unaware that you had not actually closed the front door?

You see, whilst you were busy in the kitchen, could Grace have got up and seen the door open ... and walked out?' Everyone looked a little bemused, Sam suddenly aware that it had never been picked up on before; as to who entered the room first? Sam turned to Sylvia and with a fear in her voice she started to question her, herself.

'You cooked pasta?' she suggested, sitting on the edge of the sofa.

'Yes, pasta' repeated Sylvia, her voice warbling and her nerves causing her shoulders to shake.

'Did you get to finish making the tea?' she asked.

'I don't understand?' Sylvia cried.

'Well, did you make the pasta and then call Grace or did you suddenly realise she was missing and stop cooking?' Sam stood up abruptly leaving Sylvia visibly unsettled.

Jed took over. *'The point we are trying to make Sylvia is that if you had not seen her, because you had not finished cooking her tea and thought she was safe watching Peppa and then say, she got up and thought 'oh the door is open' and wandered out, you would not have realised she had left because you, yourself were preoccupied ... you see?'*

Sylvia looked stunned and thoughts were rushing through her head. Had she finished cooking, had she called Grace or been looking behind her to see she was still on the sofa? Had she closed the front door behind them?

'*I can't remember … I can't think for a moment*' Sylvia wailed.

'*That's quite enough*' snapped Cynthia. '*I insist you leave now*' she demanded.

Sam looked to Jed, acknowledging thanks to Sylvia and agreeing to leave, hoping that a little bit of time for Sylvia would find clarification and some of the finer details could be helpful when they next speak.

The heavy front doors slammed behind them as they made their way down the concrete steps. Neither dared to look back or catch the disapproving eye of Sylvia's overprotective Mother, but in their haste to get in the car, Jed realised he had left his phone.

'*Get in, I'll go back and get it*' he said.

'*Jed*' Sam caught his arm. '*Just get it and leave quickly and quietly … please?*'

Jed grinned '*What do you take me for?*' he winked.

As he retraced his steps, he could see through the window Sylvia hugging her mother and then her chin being lifted and being reassured in a tender way.

The door opened but this time the housekeeper answered and Jed explained he had left his phone in the drawing room and before the lady could announce his arrival, Jed pushed past and entered.

As he did, he heard Cynthia telling Sylvia that it was not something she needed to worry about and there was no need to say anything.

Jed waited for a second until his presence was felt.

'*Apologies*' he said. '*I believe I left my phone*'

Cynthia was surprisingly quiet and Sylvia stunned in silence. Jed allowed the pause to be heard in the room before slowly walking over to the fireplace to retrieve it.

'*Here it is!*' he said, holding it high.

Cynthia pulled Sylvia a little closer to her side and Sylvia averted her eyes, unable to look at Jed.

He nodded, politely acknowledging their time and without any words being spoken he left the room, passing the housekeeper, who was looking quite sheepish for having allowed him entrance.

'*What took you*?' Sam asked. Jed started the car and as they drove away, he looked in his rear-view mirror to see Cynthia watching.

'*Did you find it*?' Sam asked, still waiting for a response from her first question.

'*What did you say?*' she questioned, a third time.

Jed drove for a mile or two in silence with Sam studying his expression and trying to talk to him about the timeline and the fact that Sally had been home and ….

'Jed, talk to me!'

Jed found a place to stop and pulled over. Sam undid her seatbelt and turned to face him.

'You're worrying me' she snapped.

'I didn't forget my phone' he told her. 'I just needed a reason to go back'

Sam looked a little bemused, then reminded him that he'd got in trouble in the past for that trick. It backfired once before as he had left it recording and they couldn't use the information found on it.

Then her eyes widened. 'no, not again?' Jed lowered his voice, in a way that Sam knew he was deadly serious.

'Sam, you said anything … you said you would make a deal with the Devil over and over and then thank him if need be?'. Sam stopped.

'Yes, I know … ok, what did you do?' she pleaded.

Jed told her when he arrived, he overheard Cynthia telling Sylvia that there was no need to say … 'say what?' He echoed.

There was a need to say everything, he reminded Sam and so much for them being innocent? What could possibly be a good enough reason to keep to yourself, when we are talking about a missing child?

Jed held his phone out and Sam looked down at the device, her voice trembling.

'*Do I have your permission to listen?*' he asked. Sam looked up and with tears in her eyes, she placed her hand on his phone.

'*We may not be able to use it as evidence, I realise*' continued Jed. '*But right now, we need any lead we can get?*' his voice trailed off.

Sam looked back at the phone, her hand placed on the screen. Now her voice was calm, cold even.

Raising her eyes and looking directly into his, she managed a whisper. '*Play it!*'

The two had been so thorough going over conversations and dissecting details, but with other cases to pursue Jed could not be as involved as he had been today. In fact, it had been suggested by the Police that he shouldn't get involved at all outside office hours and this had been supported by the Agency but everyone knew he would continue to pursue. The only difference was that Sam was no longer in the office every day and this left Jed with little choice but to break advice.

They did their best work together; he kept her focused when she was '*losing her shit*' and she could reign him in, when he was getting bullish.

They were both silent listening to the recap and eventually they heard themselves leaving the room and Cynthia assuring Sylvia it was over.

Jed was still looking down at his phone and listening intently when Sam gasped. Now staring at each other, Jed's expression changes to one of anger and Sam's to utter dismay as they heard a vital piece of information, not previously known.

'*I should have said at the beginning that Bryn popped round*' Sylvia cried.

'*Now then …*' soothed her mother.

'*Nothing happened that they need to worry about?*' Sylvia didn't speak but they presumed she may have nodded or whimpered quietly, as they were unable to hear.

'*One day you will bring that young man to meet me, hey?*' Cynthia cooed and this time they heard the quiet voice of agreement from Sylvia.

Seconds past and sounds of the door being knocked were heard and then Jed entering the room, only masked by Cynthia saying that there was '*no need to say anything*'.

Jed turned his phone off and looked at Sam for guidance, but she was still in shock.

'*Why? … why was this never mentioned? Who is Bryn?*' she said out loud, then with a troubled look she told Jed that there was something familiar, it was unusual, but she couldn't place it?

'*Did you know she had a boyfriend?*' asked Jed. Sam shook her head.

'*No, well not that I needed to but she knew the rules and that no-one else was allowed in the apartment. I mean, it's my home and Grace was her priority*'

Jed could only nod in agreement. '*How come the Police didn't name anyone else?*' he inquired.

'*I saw part of the transcript, read her statement later and she blatantly lied Sam?*' He was looking once more for Sam to bite, to instruct him to turn around but she was still in shock, thoughts churning.

'*Sam*' Jed broke through the awkward silence.

'*Let's go back. That fucking Mother needs shooting*' He was agitated and turned the key, forcing his foot down hard on the accelerator to increase the revs and about to go.

Sam glanced over at him. '*Wait*' she said abruptly. '*How do we know about Bryn?*' she needed to remind him. '*The recording, remember!*'

Jed gestured a so what '*We don't care about that, but we can say we want to know about him and who he is? Sam, it doesn't matter!*'

Sam was trying to think over the new information, scared she would cause a set back if they handled it wrong and today had been the most productive of all her dark days. Just a few precious hours in and they had a new lead?

Jed grabbed her hand, jolted her to look up from her stare. '*Sam, time is of the essence, please?*' he begged.

Sam could only nod, terrified that they had found something so significant, too hot to handle in a way, then terrified that they could be closer to finding out the truth and was she able to deal with it?

Jed was on a mission and drove as fast as possible, turning into the gravel drive with such force, scattering stones as he came to a halt.

It was Cynthia he noticed first as she stood pale and frozen looking out of the drawing room window. She knew and not waiting for Sam, Jed bound up the steps and hammered on the door.

It took far too long before the door was opened and when it did a hard-faced Cynthia slowly asked how she could help, but this just proved to incense Jed so he pushed past her, with Sam in tow.

Jed spun round in the hallway and demanded to speak with Sylvia again and at first Cynthia made an excuse about her being distressed and needing to rest, the request therefore being denied, but Jed shook his head, then shook his phone.

'*I don't think so, do you?*'

Cynthia looked at his phone, then to the fireplace

as she realised what had happened. With a slow exhale of breath, she called to the housekeeper and straight away the embarrassed help arrived, looking even more flustered when she saw the duo had returned.

They were asked to take a seat but declined, Sam still silent and in shock but just as Sylvia made her way down the stairs Sam's heartache became evident when she asked quietly.

'*What would you have done if it had been your family?*' Cynthia looked away; said she *was* protecting her family and surely Sam could understand that?

Sylvia entered the room, tears falling from her eyes and her cheeks reddened.

'*Who's Bryn?*' barked Jed. Sylvia's eyes shot across to her Mother, who quickly shook her head in denial

'*Not me darling, I haven't said a thing*'

Sam once again, with emotion asked the question '*Sylvia, why? You knew someone else had been there ... in my home, why wouldn't you say? For Grace?*' she cried.

Sylvia started to sob and her Mother made her sit down on the sofa, whilst she sat on the arm and placed her own around her daughter's shoulders once more.

'*I promise you Sam, Grace was safe, she was*

watching tv, she was safe. I promise' Sylvia leaned forward and begged Sam to believe her.

'*Who is Bryn?*' Jed asked once more. '*Who the fuck is Bryn?*' Sam swung round and raised her hand in the air.

'*Jed, please'*. Jed walked away towards the window but his muttering could still be heard.

'*Who is he Sylvia?*' Sam asked softly, trying to keep her emotions in check. '*Your boyfriend? Has he popped round before?*' she persisted.

Sylvia looked to her Mother and for a moment it felt like she didn't wish to talk openly, not in front of Cynthia anyhow, but unfortunately so much time had been wasted and Sam could not let this moment pass so she pushed Sylvia for an explanation, either here or at the Station and then there was the matter of her statement?

Sylvia gasped, then sat up in her seat. '*Not a boyfriend, though we love each other*' she started to explain. '*On a Tuesday and Thursday, he pops round to see me, not for long mind*' she once more glanced up at her Mother, then back to Sam hoping for the acknowledgement of her belief and to bring the conversation to an end.

'*Ok*' accepted Sam, though this was far from ok. '*Pops round? To mine? While you are looking after Grace?*' this time Sam smiled, hoping to relax her into opening up a little more and talking freely.

Sylvia nodded. '*Yes, he pops round because he finishes work early on a Tuesday so we get a little longer and I know I shouldn't let him come to yours but he is kind and so good with Grace*' Sylvia started to smile, obviously very fond of Bryn.

'*He reads to her sometimes, when I'm cooking*' she continued. '*He's so good with children and he's so kind to me*'

Jed was walking back towards the women, it was evident that he was breathing in and out with a great deal of control, keeping his tone even and started with an apology for barking, for which Sylvia felt better for hearing.

'*So, Bryn came round that Tuesday?*' he suggested. Sylvia was about to agree but Jed continued. '*I am guessing that is why you went in the apartment first, with the pushchair and Grace behind?*' he drew a deeper breath '*because Bryn would be at the back, last one in as it were?*'

Sylvia nodded, '*Yes, I would leave the door ajar if he was coming but always, always watching for Grace*' she added.

'*We need to talk with him*' said Sam but immediately Sylvia rose from her seat and begged them to please let her speak with him first. This got shut down by Jed instantly and his voice grew louder before Cynthia managed to put a halt to the interrogation, as she saw it.

'*This has been gruelling enough*' she stated. '*Please Sam, just allow Sylvia to speak with him and for him to contact you?*' she looked between the two of them and Jed's response was an emphatic no, but Sam looked at Sylvia, a young woman she had known for a few years and their families had been connected via their Mothers. She felt sure still that Sylvia had been an innocent victim in all of this but Bryn was so important a factor she couldn't consider waiting. Grace was missing, too much time had already passed.

'*Please?*' begged Sylvia once more. '*I will ask him to speak with you in the morning, first thing*' she pleaded.

To Jed's surprise Sam agreed, encouraging her colleague to leave without saying anything else but the second they got in the car and sped away Jed's verbal outrage was loud and clear.

As they arrived at Sam's apartment block, things had calmed down a little, though Jed could not understand how Sam was allowing the moment to pass?

'*Sam, snap out of it!*' he yelled. '*For fucks sake, he is a key witness, what are we waiting for?*'

Sam asked him to get out of the car and as they stepped inside the foyer, Jed opened his arms and gestured '*now what?*'

'*You saw for yourself the CCTV outside, didn't*

you?' Jed nodded. '*Yeah*?' then questioned where this was going.

'*I remembered that when we watched it, the only people coming and going that day into the block were accounted for, tenants, some of their families, couple of friends, even a delivery guy I remember*' Jed butted in, '*Yeah, so?*'

'*So, it got me thinking*?' Sam continued '*We watched as Sylvia walked in with Grace and she was pushing the buggy in one hand, holding Grace's hand with the other, right*?' Jed stopped, he suddenly caught up with Sam and finished her sentence. '*So, Bryn, whoever he is, did not walk in with her?*'

Sam nodded, eyes wide and smiling. '*Exactly, he must have already been here, or living here and she also said 'pop round' so then I thought I know that name, it's unusual so rather than wait for her to talk with him I wanted to get back to see if I was right'.*

Sam turned to the mail boxes against the wall and next to hers was her neighbour's box Mr B Edwards.

'*B for Bryn?*' she suggested.

'*How old is he?*' came Jed's reply.

'*Old enough to know better I'm thinking*?' said Sam and with that Jed turned to head up the staircase, with Sam in hot pursuit.

'*Jed, wait*' Sam lowered her voice. '*Listen, I don't know my neighbours, not really, I'm hardly home but I do know he has a teenage daughter and I am sure she is deaf, so please be thoughtful for her sake?'* Jed looked back at Sam and nodded though she felt that would only serve to help the girl, perhaps not her father.

Jed knocked on the door, then once again and finally a third time.

'What time did she say he finished work?' Sam looked at her watch and realised it was a Wednesday, so they were unsure.

'We need to talk to him before Sylvia does' said Jed.

'Ideally' agreed Sam, but as they spoke the door at the end of the hallway opened and peeping out was Sally. Jed turned his attentions to her and before Sam had a chance to grab him, he marched over.

'So, you know what's going on, eh?' he snapped *'Good with details huh?'* Sam was close behind now and pulled at his jacket, stopping him from getting even closer.

Sally pulled open her door and with a cigarette hanging from her lip she pulled up her sleeve to her elbow and gave a slight grin.

'Oh, let the boy try' she groaned. *'I ain't done nothing wrong!'* Jed again raised his voice.

'Seriously?' he shouted. *'Withholding information is a crime, you stupid old bat!'* Sam thumped Jed hard *'enough!'*

Jed turned back, passing Sam, leaving her to step a little closer to Sally.

'*Why didn't you say Sylvia's boyfriend had been round? Do you know him?*' Sally looked past her to see where Jed had gone, then looked back at Sam and flicked ash on the floor by her feet.

'*I'm not guilty of anything girl, so don't start wagging that finger at me*' Sally started to wave her arms about and gesturing with her head in a feisty, argumentative manner.

'*They asked me if I had seen anyone and I said no, other than Sylvia and the baby and that was the truth!*'

'*But we were told you weren't in, yet you clearly were?*' Sam asked. '*I told them I wasn't in when the baby went missing and that was true, but I had seen them on their way into the building as I was heading out! They didn't ask me that*', she said defiantly.

Sam looked back at Jed who was now leaning on the bannisters and although frustrated, was a little calmer.

'*... apology accepted!*' Sally retorted, then with the same defiance, she slammed the door in Sam's face.

Sam walked back to Jed. '*Come inside*' she said and touched his elbow to encourage him.

Once inside she slumped down in the chair and took the longest, deepest breath she could manage, before exhaling just as hard.

'*What a day*' she heard herself say. '*But in one day Jed, you have unravelled things. I am forever in your debt*' she said. '*I only wish we had worked together like this, earlier*' Jed stopped her mid-sentence and held his finger out.

'*Sam, the woulda, shoulda, coulda shit will consume you*' He continued. '*Don't do it. We were working together every day in the office, but we got a lucky break today*'

He then joined her in the seat opposite and slumped down, placing his feet higher on the pouffe.

'*You know I had three main cases at the time and you and I worked hard night after night 'til the early hours trying to fit it all*' he was trying to smile a little and eventually he received one back from Sam, for she knew he was right, they had put in all the hours, exhausted all resources available.

'*You're right, I know*' Sam said, her face a little more like he remembered, calm and warm, for today had been positive and they had a potential new lead.

A few coffees later and the crazy wall had been updated. Jed was concerned that Sylvia would get to speak with Bryn first but it was out of their control; he had a teenage daughter so they felt confident she would have to come home at some point.

When they heard her walking up the stairs Sam refused to let Jed approach her for fear of her Father blowing up in their faces; they needed to give him the chance to explain.

Finally, there was a tap on her door and Jed rushed ahead to answer. In front of him stood a burly man, in his mid to late 40s and slightly unkempt. Sam stood by Jed's side as he introduced himself as Bryn and pinching Jed's shirt at the back as a reminder not to react, Jed shook his hand and asked if he could answer a few questions.

To their surprise Bryn agreed instantly, but suggested they do it inside and not in his own apartment, where his daughter was doing her homework.

This was not exactly how things should be done and so far, Sam and Jed were piling through information as they found it, not handing it on to the Police, not looking at statements or requesting things to be re-examined.

Sam was on a mission to find Grace; she had been forced to take leave and was supposed to step back from the case but that was never going to happen. In fact, it was Jed who risked his job today, a decision he said he could live with.

As Bryn entered the room, he couldn't help but notice the wall adorned with photographs and information. He swallowed hard and said he was so sorry to hear of Grace still missing, that she was adorable and he would do anything he could to help.

'*Why were you not in Sylvia's statement*? Jed started. Bryn looked at the two of them, unsure as to who was in charge and oblivious to the fact that Sam was temporarily absent from the Agency.

'*Look at me*?' came his reply, his voice slow and gravelly.

'*She said her Mother wouldn't understand our relationship, so we're just friends*' he said but his eyes kept darting between the two as if to be searching for the more sympathetic one.

'*A child went missing*?' Jed said in a tone that asked him if he actually realised the seriousness of the situation, apart from his own selfish desire to keep out of the headlines.

'*I know, I realise that*' Bryn continued. '*I told Sylvia not to lie and I knew there would be evidence of me being here. I mean, DNA ... it would show there was someone else here, wouldn't it?*'

Sam looked puzzled, then queried aloud '*That's a point, why did that not come out*?' she asked.

'*It did*' Bryn replied. '*They asked Sylvia, in fact they told her someone else was here as there was proof .... '*

Bryn paused, feeling uncomfortable. '*Erm*' he stumbled, then picked up the pace again.

'*They badgered her and she eventually told them I had been here. They came to see me and eliminated me from their enquiry?*' he confirmed.

'*Why wasn't I told someone else had been in my apartment?*' snapped Sam.

'*I believe it was Sylvia's Mother who asked for that to be kept out, once they had decided there was no question of my innocence?*' Bryn raised his shoulders in question.

'*Honestly, I thought you must have known by now but she sounds like a formidable woman so I guess she has more power than I gave her credit for*'. Bryn then shook his head. '*Now I get it, why Sylvia said her Mother would never understand about us?*'

Sam stood up and paced. '*No, she would not!*' she barked. '*In fact, you are the polar opposite of what she wants for her daughter. Do yourself a favour and run for the hills because if she is capable of controlling something like this, you have no chance!*'

Jed was still staring at Bryn, studying his body language and unable to quite let go of his words. '*You were going to say something*? He said, calm and slow.

'*Huh?*' replied Bryn.

'*You paused, said something about there would be proof of someone having been here?*' Jed continued.

Bryn looked taken aback and glanced over at Sam, then back to Jed.

'*Where?*' Jed leaned forward '*Where was the proof?*'

Jed leant further forward, his elbows on his knees and his head resting in his hand, his voice commanding.

'*You leave the room Bryn, leave Grace watching tv and what? ... to the bedroom for a kiss and cuddle?*'

Sam squealed '*No way!*' but Jed stopped her as she rushed to Bryn, who by now raising his hands to protect himself.

'*In my apartment?*' screamed Sam '*With my granddaughter here?*'

Bryn still had his arms out in front to protect himself.

'*I followed her into the bedroom when she put Grace's laundry away, that was all. I sat on the bed whilst she did that and I think I pulled her down for a quick kiss, that's all. We could hear the tv and Grace was watching Peppa and eating pasta, nothing else*'

Sam threw a cushion at his head, unable to reach him herself and Jed pointed to the seat beside him. '*Sam, sit, we're getting somewhere, please?*'

For the first time the tables were turned and Sam was being reigned in. She had entrusted Sylvia to look after Grace until she got home and then she would watch Grace for the last hour before her Mum came to collect her. It worked! It worked so well and the three generations shared precious time. But here, in the sanctity of her own home, where Grace should have been safe, she was neglected.

'*You left a 2-year-old alone*?' Sam started to whimper; a tear dropped to her cheek.

'*And I will never forgive myself*' said Bryn, his head low and his hand on his chest, placed across his heart. Bryn stood up.

'*I will be checking with the Police and reading your statement; no matter what power Cynthia thinks she has and Bryn ...* 'Bryn looked up, alerted by Jed's tone.

'*I will be talking to you in front of your daughter and believe me, deaf or not, she will understand, trust me*' Bryn nodded furiously. '*Now get out!*'

As Bryn made his way to the door, he stumbled over Jed's boots.

'*Wait*' called out Sam. '*How did you know we wanted to talk to you? Sylvia?*'

Bryn shook his head '*No ... Sally called me at work*' he said.

'*What is the deal with Sally?*' she asked. Bryn had his hand on the door and was about to open it but stopped briefly to explain that for the last 5 years, since he had been on his own with his daughter, Sally had been kind enough to keep an eye out for her when she came home from school, until he got home.

They had a light that flashed inside the apartment to alert her when there was someone at the door but she was under strict instructions not to answer the door when he was out. Sally used to listen out for visitors, head them off, or more likely confront them and send them packing.

'*Kindness from Sally?*' jibed Jed. '*That doesn't fit?*' Bryn tipped his head to one side and gave a wry smile.

'*Well, I mean I keep her topped up with fags and booze, it's what she asked for?*'

Jed glanced over to Sam '*Yep, that's the price of being neighbourly these days!*' and with that Bryn pulled the door.

'*Listen I better get home Sam, are you going to be alright?*' Jed walked over to her and pulled her into his arms, giving her a squeeze and joking with her that she needed a shower desperately. Sam broke free and thumped him on the arm '*Git*' she giggled and watched as he headed for the door.

Jed bent down to put on his boots and Sam told him she may actually sleep a little tonight and tomorrow they would return to Sylvia and Cynthia if need be, head to the Station to clarify things and see what else they could uncover.

'*I think I better go to the Station*' Jed explained. '*You are on leave remember?*' Sam sighed, realising it made sense.

'... and listen Sam, I know I have to get home now but call me, please don't lock me out?' Sam agreed. 'Say hi to Lisa and hug those boys for me'.

Jed chuckled 'I tell you, 5-year old boys, now that takes it out of you! I think Lisa is secretly looking forward to returning to work but childcare costs will break the bank'

Sam interrupted him 'Don't be in a rush to hand them over' she said. Jed opened the door, before looking back at her

'No, I feel your pain, if only a little Sam. Night mate'

Sam laid down on the sofa, exhausted, information overload and aches in her body she never knew possible. Yes, she did stink ... perhaps a bath?

A call broke her relaxation and Sam hurried to reach for her phone, water slowly dripping off her hand and a few bubbles on her screen quickly blown away.

'Mum?' came a familiar voice. Sam closed her eyes.

'Hello darling' she said as she laid back in the bath. 'How are you?'

Mia started the conversation slowly and the two discussed Mia's work, her marriage, then her Mum's enforced leave which was news to Mia and finally the elephant in the room – Grace.

'You should have told me' said Mia. *'I have been so horrible to you, distant too, but I don't know how to deal with any of this'*

Sam reassured her daughter that no-one knows how to handle something like this; it's not real to be fair. It's full of what ifs and maybes, then a new lead, more hope and total fear in equal amounts. There is no rule book, just tears and woes and a small heartbeat of hope that stays with you until the end.

Sam didn't want to stress Mia out any further but today had been such a positive day she wanted to share with her daughter the new hope she had, small snippets and thankfully Mia held on to that too.

She giggled for the first time, she cried of course, but Sam could hear her voice lift and the two were close again, momentarily.

'How's Joe doing' Sam asked. Mia sighed and for a split-second Sam wished she hadn't asked. He had been a difficult one to handle as Mia's success had taken off but he still spent money as though it was in excess and to keep him upbeat Mia had turned a blind eye.

'We have been apart for a few months now' she said. Sam sat up in the bath, waves of water and bubbles rushed over her legs, over the side and onto the floor.

'*No! You should have called*?' Sam felt a weight of guilt as she realised, she hadn't known.

'*We're both the same*' Mia commented. '*You having to walk away from your life essentially and keeping that away from me and I'm doing something similar by keeping further pain from you*'

Sam dared to mention their angel's name '*There's no pain like losing Grace*' she said and the two were quiet in their private heartache. '*No, nothing will ever hurt me again*' agreed Mia.

Day 2 - Thursday

The following morning took Sam by surprise. She slept all night and by the time she woke, she had overslept for two hours.

Up, dressed and coffee in hand, Sam checked her phone before leaving and saw a message from Jed to say he loved working with her yesterday and that he would give her a call around lunchtime. He also mentioned he would be heading to the Station later that morning and would see if there were any more inconsistencies and would update her. She held the phone to her chest and gave a comforting sigh.

Pulling the door behind her, Sam turned to lock it and right on cue, 'Sally down the alley', made an appearance.

'*Morning*' Sam managed to say through gritted teeth. Sally waved a hand and closed the door.

Before she could drop the key into her bag, the slamming of another door shook the building as Jose's partner marched towards her, glaring as he brushed past and rushed down the stairs.

Sam looked over the bannister and watched as he pulled aside the heavy door and stepped out onto the street.

She waited for a second, looked to see if Sally's door

was closed, then headed for the door that was still shaking on its hinges. She tapped gently, looking around carefully in the hope of not alerting Sally.

Sam whispered *'Jose? I'm Sam, I live a couple of doors along'* then she waited. *'Jose, are you there?'* she tried again. A few minutes had passed and Sam decided to leave it, hoping not to cause any problems for the young woman but just as she stepped aside the door opened slightly and again with the chain between them, Jose peeked past.

'Hi my name's Sam, Are you ok?' Jose nodded, her face was dirty and she too was in need of a shower.

Then Sam noticed there was blood on her hand and further down, on her long tee shirt. *'You hurt?'* Sam asked but with that Jose glanced down and closed the door fast.

Sam leaned against the door. *'listen, please. I can help you. I can protect you?'* This time no answer, Sam hoped she was on the other side listening so she bent down and whispered that she could trust her for help and could arrange a refuge where she would be safe and could have a better life.

Still no reply so Sam said she would go, but meant what she said. She would like to help.

A small piece of paper appeared underneath the door, slightly crumpled with a stain on it and a bloody finger print across the middle. The note read:

'*They took her*'. Sam cupped her mouth with her hand so as not to scream out loud, but then tapped the door again.

'*Who, Jose? Grace? Our Grace? Who took her?*' she whispered but as emotion got the better of her, she realised she was talking a little loud and realised Sally's door was opening. Sam turned quickly and headed down the stairs but just a few steps down, she stopped and sat for a moment to compose herself. Tears ran down her face and one dripped onto the piece of paper that she held so tenderly, its importance too much to bear.

Suddenly the foyer doors burst open and in strutted Jose's partner, his swagger personified and as he climbed the first staircase. Sam rose quickly placing the piece of paper in her pocket and passing him as they turned the corner.

He stopped, smirked at her; his stinking wet breath on her lips as he spat. '*What?*' he sniped. '*You're one of those do-gooders aren't ya? No tough boyfriend around today?*' He laughed. '*He needs to mind his own business!*'

Sam was unable to react, frozen, but not from fear. Aware that this note could be incriminating and she could be staring into the face of the monster that took Grace, that she was so close she could literally smell him and all she could think was that she must keep walking, so she did with each step weighing her down. She was vaguely aware he was still calling out to her, insulting her probably, but she kept walking, her ears buzzing.

Eventually she pulled open the heavy resisting doors and embraced the street air, as if oxygen to her lungs.

Pulling out her phone Sam tried to text Jed but her fingers were not willing so she started to walk through crowds, bumping into bodies, then a bag or briefcase, watching as people moaned that she wasn't looking where she was going.

Her car was in the lower basement car park but Sam couldn't even think how to get there, instead a black cab was heading towards her and without thinking she hailed it.

The Police Station would have been the place to go but in her daze, she headed for Jed's home and when his wife Lisa opened the door, she fell into her arms before being pulled swiftly inside.

Lisa held Sam close. She knew how important her relationship with Jed was, but never fearing anything untoward between them. Their age difference was enough but Jed never gave her an ounce of worry where Sam was concerned. They were so close that Sam had been made a Godmother to the boys and over the years they had spent a lot of social time together so when Jed said he was emotionally involved with Grace too, he meant it.

'*Sam, what's wrong?*' Lisa took her to one side and tried to raise Sam's chin. Her face wet with tears and she was making no sense at all, trying to talk, crying and breathing at the same time.

Eventually Lisa managed to get through to Sam and once Sam had quietened down, Lisa walked her to the kitchen.

'*The boys are at School; do you want me to drive you to the Agency?*' Lisa asked. '*Shall I call Jed?*'

Sam slurred her words, holding out her hand to suggest that she needed a moment more, then pulled the note from her bag.

Lisa looked at it closely, trying to smooth out the crumpled paper as she focused.

'*Who are **they**?*' she asked, her eyes wide with surprise '*They took Grace? Is that what this means?*'

Sam nodded as Lisa started to mix her words, talk faster and pacing the kitchen.

'*Oh my God, we must call Jed*' she insisted.

'*No, please don't, not yet*' Sam begged. '*I couldn't think, just jumped in a cab, I'm sorry*'

Lisa gave Sam a hug '*Never be sorry, you are always welcome here, you know that*' Lisa sat on the breakfast stool opposite.

'*So, tell me, where did you find the note?*' she asked.

Sam explained she had been passed it by the neighbour, very likely a domestic violence victim and to be honest she wasn't sure why she had been given it but it was like a bolt from the blue and suddenly she was holding a time bomb; not sure whether to run with it or throw it; but in her hands she could be holding the vital piece?

'Tomorrow will be 6 months to the day Lisa' Sam said quietly. '6 months!' Lisa placed her hand on Sam's

'I know. We haven't stopped talking about her, every day Jed goes over and over things but he told me yesterday was amazing?' Lisa opened her eyes wide and tried to encourage Sam to talk.

'Come on, it was one thing after another eh? The little things Sam, enough to get Jed on the scent anyway?!' she giggled and Sam smiled in return.

Lisa was in her mid-30s and willingly gave up her job to look after their boys, having tried for a few years to conceive, then finding out there were two, it was a precious time they didn't wish to miss out on.

Jed's work was so erratic, Lisa was well aware that any child care would fall on her so it made practical and financial sense to be a stay at home Mum.

Lisa tried once more to persuade Sam to call Jed and again was reminded that she was not allowed to be involved in the case. She didn't feel able to let this piece of paper go to anyone else and intended to return to Jose and put a little pressure on her, but knew the risk to them both and possibly Grace if he was to catch them.

They talked for a good hour before Sam said she felt calmer and thanked Lisa for listening, finally agreeing to keep Jed out of the loop for the rest of the day.

   'Let him come home' Sam pleaded *'He was due to call me around lunchtime, after he had been to the Station but if I showed him this he would charge right in and I just feel Jose is too fragile, she could be the key witness here, you know?'* Lisa agreed but said Jed would be furious, he would say you never go in alone and Sam knew that.

   'I just want to talk with her first, that's all' she said as she stepped outside the door. *'I need to make sure she's safe, otherwise I may be left with just this scrap of paper and no witness?'*

They hugged and agreed Jed would call Sam later in the day.

On the taxi ride back to the apartment Sam tried to remember if she had seen Jose's partner leave regularly at a certain time on any particular day but she couldn't recall. They would need to know his name, do some digging, but most importantly Sam needed access to Jose.

She knew he had passed her on the staircase on

his way back to the apartment earlier but how to find out if he was still inside? That was going to be tricky … *but then?*

Tapping on Sally's door wasn't her first choice but the most obvious and Sally didn't rush when opening up either. But when she did, she cocked her head to one side and made a sly remark along the lines of '*Oh, need me now eh?*'

'*Yes Sally*' cooed Sam '*You really could do me a favour?*' she said, pampering to her every word.

'*What do you want?*' came the curt reply.

'*Did you see Jose's partner go into the apartment earlier?*' asked Sam.

'*When you left?*' Sally asked, again with a sideways glance

'*Yes, when I left, he passed me on the stairs, but do you know if he went out again, after that?*'

'*So, basically, you just want to know if he's in?*' asked Sally in her matter-of-fact tone.

'*Exactly*' agreed Sam '*Is he home?*' Sally held out her hand

'*What's in it for me?*' she said and as Sam hadn't anything to offer in the way of goods, she pulled out her purse. There were a couple of notes tucked inside and just as she was pulling out the brown £10 Sally sniggered, saying '*don't be stingy*' and pointed to the £20.

Reluctantly Sam passed the larger note and once more asked her to clarify, *for certain*, if he was home or not? *'Yeah, he's home'* she said and suddenly the door at the opposite end of the hallway opened, slammed loudly and they both watched as he spat on the ground at the top of the stairs and grinned at them both before disappearing once more from the building.

Sam put out her hand *'… that's answered that then?'* she said thinking Sally would return the money but Sally pulled her hand inside the door sharply, muttering *'Let me know if I can be of further help?'*

With that and unsure how long he was going to be out Sam made her way to Jose's door.

She tapped again and asked Jose to open but no answer. She nearly said out loud that she needed to know more about the note but had a moment of panic when she wondered whether Jose was there alone? She whispered for her to please open the door.

She hadn't really thought Jose would dare to do so, but she did. Sam gushed 'thank you' to her as the chain crossed in front of her face.

'Please Jose, I need to know?' begged Sam, shaking the note. *'Is this about my granddaughter Grace? Who took her?'*

Jose kept looking past Sam and this caused Sam to feel unnerved and look back over her own shoulder. The outside door downstairs was very heavy and a little noisy so Sam assured Jose they would hear if anyone arrived.

'*I can't talk*' said Jose, tears welling up in her eyes. '*He could come back at any time*'

Sam placed her fingers across the chain '*I know, I know*' she said. '*I am listening and you could tell me really quickly and I'll go?*'

Jose looked Sam in the eyes, she could see the desperation and for Jose, Sam's kindness was something long since craved. No-one showed her any such thought and although they were relative strangers Jose felt moved by her words.

'*Yes*' she finally caved. '*Your friend brought her here that day and Rick said she would just be staying for a couple of hours?*' Sam reeled back

'*My friend?*' she exclaimed. '*What friend?*'

'*The man that comes here*' she said. Sam still looked surprised.

'*The man I was with yesterday?*'

Jose stopped to think '*Maybe*' she said. '*He was holding her and they came in, told me to play with her for a couple of hours and then she would be going home?*'

'*I think you're mistaken?*' Sam replied '*Jed was at work with me that day, when Grace went missing?*'

'*He was here, I'm telling you; he came in with Rick and they said to play with her while they talked business'*

Sam stepped back slightly, unable to process. A large creak downstairs caused Jose to gasp *'Go, go'* she said and very discreetly closed the door leaving Sam to walk away, confused and once more in a daze.

Rick bound back up the stairs then came to a complete stop as he watched Sam heading back to her door. There was only one empty apartment between the two so he glanced at his door, then at Sam.

'You been to mine?' he barked.

'No' said Sam, trying to keep her composure. *'Thought I heard someone next door, in the empty apartment'* she said quickly. *'Have you seen anyone go in?'* she said immediately after. *'I checked with Sally earlier, but she hadn't seen anyone. I am telling you there is definitely noise coming from there'* and with that she placed her ear against the door.

'That why you were pestering Sally earlier?' he asked. Sam opened her door

'Not pestering, just doing the neighbourly thing' she commented and stepped inside.

Sam closed her door and looking through the peep hole watched as Rick headed for their neighbour's door and she could just see as he placed his eye close to the peep hole. She prayed that it was enough for him to believe and that she hadn't put

Jose in danger, for her own sake but more importantly for Grace. A second later his apartment door slammed shut, the vibration being felt along the hallway.

By lunchtime Sam was in turmoil and by the time Jed called Sam could hardly bare to answer the phone. Eventually a voicemail was left and Jed explained how Bryn's statement had checked out and the Police had eliminated him from their enquiries.

He also said that he would finish work and head over before going home and that Sam needed to check in.

Sam curled up on the sofa, her knees tucked underneath and a cushion being held tightly against her chest.

She couldn't get the words out of her head, but even with a mix up Jed was not at the property that fateful day. No way, he had been at work!

Lastly Sylvia would not have been in trouble if she had said Jed had been there and Cynthia would certainly not have allowed him to be so hard on them, if they had something on him? He had not been seen on the CCTV entering or leaving the property either. This was crazy nonsense and Jose had definitely got it wrong … it had to be wrong?

By 5pm Sam was still curled up, hadn't moved and the night was drawing in. No lights were on when

Jed knocked on the door; he tapped and called for Sam to answer but for a moment she was frozen.

Watching the door, she couldn't move; her mind still trying to filter the facts, yet recalling Jed saying *'it's usually someone close, someone you trust and wouldn't suspect'* haunted her.

Her phone started to ring and Sam leant forward in a rush to pick it up from the table and silence it, but Jed called out.

'Sam, open up. I heard your phone!' he sounded frustrated.

Sam made her way to the door and immediately he asked what was wrong, moving her to one side as he squeezed past. Closing the door, he said he wasn't going to move one inch until she talked.

Yesterday had been such a high and today her world had been split. She did say she would do a deal with the Devil, would do anything she had to for Grace to be safe but now she was looking in the face of the impossible and the one person she would have turned to had become a suspect.

Jed denied all knowledge and yes, he had been at work that day. What concerned him was why did Jose give Sam a note, lead her to believe she knew something, then make up a pack of lies?

'I went to yours earlier' Sam confessed.

'Mine?' asked Jed. *'To see Lisa?'* he continued.

'Yeah, I just got in a taxi and went to yours, you were at work and I couldn't disturb you but Lisa was amazing. In fact, she said to call you, but I said no, so don't give her a hard time ok'

'I won't, I'm glad she helped but Sam, please tell me you believe me? I did not have anything to do with Grace being taken?'

Sam lowered her eyes 'I'm going mad Jed, forgive me?'

Jed stepped forward and held her.

'We'll get there, don't worry' he assured her. 'But Sam, I need to talk to Jose ... please don't let this fester, we need to know what that was all about or at least confirm it wasn't me?'

Sam agreed but they would have to wait for Rick to leave and in his line of work, he was in and out often. Work may be lucrative, but definitely not legal.

Jed called Lisa, saying he would be home a little later than planned and when Rick next left the building Sam and Jed headed to his apartment, with one of them keeping watch over the balcony and the other tapping on the door.

This time it opened a little faster and Jose gasped again

'You can't keep coming here' she said, panic in her voice, infused with fear.

'It's ok, just a quick yes or no ok' Sam said and then moved aside so Jose could see Jed at the top of the stairs. 'Is that him?'

Jose looked past the chain, 'That's not the man with Grace; the other man' she insisted.

'What other man?' Sam begged, relief flooding through her tone 'Please Jose, we need to find the other man? Who is he? Do you mean Bryn, my neighbour?'

Jose shook her head 'No, he has a key 'cos he told Rick that he could get in and out without being heard. Now, please … I have to go'

The door closed and Sam walked over to Jed who only managed to catch a little of what Jose was saying but relieved that he was no longer a suspect.

'A key?' he repeated. 'Who has a key?

Sam and Jed returned to her apartment and she reminded him that there were only 3 keys, she had one, Mia had one and Sylvia had one.

Jed grabbed a glass of water and gulped it down. 'Wait, hang on' he said. 'What about Joe?'

'Joe?' echoed Sam, her voice trailing off a little. 'Joe has only been to mine a handful of times, when I couldn't get back in time. He's only collected her a couple of times so he has no need for a key?' then she thought about it.

'Then he would have used Mia's key?' suggested Jed, but Sam knew that if he was taking over from Sylvia there would be no need for a key as she would be there?

A quick telephone call to Sylvia confirmed that on the couple of occasions she could remember Joe collecting Grace, he definitely used a key. Sam and Jed were left silenced.

There was another tap on the door and Sam went ahead of Jed to investigate.

As she opened the door, she was surprised to see Bryn standing before her, his hands fidgeting.

'*Bryn*?' she questioned. Bryn coughed nervously.

'*Hi*' he cleared his throat. '*Sorry to disturb you*' and by the time he had finished the sentence Jed had joined them at the door.

'*Hi*' he nodded to Jed.

'*How can I help?*' Sam asked. '*We're in the middle of something*'

Bryn coughed once more, took a deep breath and asked if he could come in. Begrudgingly Sam stood aside and allowed him to enter.

Bryn turned to face them and with uncomfortable stature he started by saying he knows Sally would be watching and the last thing he needed was for her to gossip.

'*About what?*' Sam snapped. '*Bryn, we really*

don't have time to waste' she said *'What is it?'*

Bryn started to explain that his daughter was not aware of his friendship with Sylvia and whenever they met, he made sure no physical contact was shown.

Sam and Jed looked bewildered and waited for him to continue which he did once he realised, they were not interested in his personal life.

'Well, I have never spoken to my daughter Gabby about little Grace missing as I try hard to protect; you don't realise the difficulty in dealing with an upset child who cannot fully understand your explanation, the reality of your worry, when you are gesturing or signing'

Sam nodded emphatically *'Ok'* she said *'But now you have?'* she asked, in the vain hope that there was something enlightening to follow.

'Well ...' continued Bryn, *'when I got home yesterday, she was looking at the paper and pointed to the photograph of Grace, asking me if it was who she thought it was and ... well, I really didn't want to go there but she got upset when she found out I had kept it from her'* Bryn perched on the breakfast stool and his voice broke as he pulled a hanky from his pocket and wiped his nose.

'Bryn' pressed Sam with haste *'have you got information?'* Jed leaned against the same breakfast bar and to Sam's surprise he tapped Bryn's

forearm gently and spoke

'*Come on mate, we know it was tough but you came here for a reason, what was it?*'

Bryn cleared his throat again '*We talked it over and I tried to explain the date, 6 months ago is a long time for her to think back to but then that didn't matter as she said something that got me thinking and Sylvia has never mentioned it before*'

Jed waved his hand '*Yeah, go on …*' he gestured.

'*Grace's Dad?*' he said and with that he frowned with a questionable expression

'*Gabby told me he sometimes picks her up? Sylvia never mentioned him before; crazy right?*'

Sam walked back a little and pushed the front door closed, then walked past the two men and paced a little ahead before turning back to front Bryn.

'*Are you saying that Gabby remembered that day or that Joe, Grace's Dad, picked her up that day?*'

Bryn was shaking his head vehemently '*No, no*' he was moving his arms side to side. '*That's what I mean, the Police didn't speak with Gab because she had been at school so couldn't offer any information, but she told me she remembered him taking her one day and when I asked why that stuck in her mind she said it was because she was coming home from school when she spotted him coming down the fire escape at the end … ?*' Bryn pointed to the right of Sam's apartment, along the corridor to the fire escape which was next to Jose and Rick's apartment at the end.

Sam and Jed stared at each other. *'Fire escape?'* repeated Jed. *'She is certain she saw them coming down the fire escape?'*

Bryn nodded; his eyes wider than usual *'Yeah, I asked her a few times and then she asked me why it was such a big deal and I had to explain fully that Grace had been taken and we talked about the newspaper report'* Bryn paused *'She sobbed. She sobbed so much bless her, saying she had seen them, Grace in her Dad's arms and Rick. They were coming down the fire escape as she was crossing over to the apartment'*

Sam paced over to the wall and Jed walked over to join her, leaving Bryn waiting.

He called out to them *'That's new information, right?'* he asked *'Did the Police think about the fire escape? They must have, surely?'*

Jed looked back at Bryn and confirmed everywhere had been checked but it was the fact that the apartment had not been broken into, that Sylvia had been looking after her that seemed to dictate their detailed search, that CCTV did not show her leaving through the doors but unfortunately there's no coverage of the fire escapes.

Jed thanked Bryn for his time and especially for talking with Gabby. He walked towards him and shook his hand before seeing him out.

He then asked Bryn to keep that information to himself, adding. *'Not even Sylvia?'* he insisted. *'Just for now, keep it close?'* Bryn was more than happy to keep that to himself, not only did it exonerate him further but it was a contribution towards his taking liberties and spending time in Sam's apartment.

Jed returned to Sam's side and placed his hand on her shoulder causing her to look up at him, her eyes a little teary, but her demeanour calm.

'So, tell me' she whispered to him. *'How do I tell my daughter that her baby's Father may be involved?'*

Jed took a moment to let that sink in but before he had a moment to filter, he heard himself say that once again; someone you trust. Sam closed her eyes.

They agreed it would make sense for Sam to pop round to Mia when she finished work. She told her last night that she and Joe had separated, but what on earth was he thinking? Why did he take Grace? What the hell had happened but then a moment of elation flooded her veins.

'Jed' she beamed *'At least we know she will be alright? If Joe took her, for whatever reason, he wouldn't let anything happen to her'* she giggled as continued in a state of euphoria. *'Oh, thank God, it was probably to spite Mia, you know, with their separating and he has been so against her being a part-*

time Mum that this is his twisted way of getting back at her'

Jed nodded but felt Sam's enthusiasm was perhaps a little premature; however, he couldn't allow that to detract from the small amount of hope she was celebrating.

'I can't breathe' she gasped and reached her hand out for Jed to support her which he did, encouraging her to sit for a moment.

'Just shock' he assured her *'a little light-headed'*

Later that evening Sam made her way to Mia's house, pulling the car into the driveway but then realising she had company.

The doorbell rang and Mia stepped back in surprise when she saw her mother standing there.

'Oh no!' she cried and placed her hands over her mouth, but Sam quickly pulled them down *'No, no, nothing like that'* she said and pulled Mia into her arms.

'What is it then?' Mia asked as she righted herself.

'I needed to talk with you, just to go through the latest information I had, that's all … You have company?' Sam pointed to the cars covering the driveway and at the end of her garden. Mia nodded

'Yeah, business I don't need right now' she

slammed. *'I cannot believe I have to make small talk when my child is out there somewhere!'*

Sam told her it was better to be busy and distracted, but she could not help wondering how Mia was able to get herself all dolled up and prepare for an evening of entertainment when she herself was struggling to have a shower after 6 days and had to be forced to clear up her apartment and wash!

'Listen, on second thoughts, I won't come in' Sam added *'If you could just let me have an address for Joe, I want talk to him'*

'Joe?' inquired Mia. *'What's the update then?'* Sam saw people milling around behind Mia and making their way from the kitchen to the dining room with wine so she took the moment to step back a little further.

'I just need to check a couple of time line dates with you both but I am happy to catch you tomorrow and I will run them past Joe tonight?'

That appeared to throw Mia off for the scent and she accepted her Mother's explanation. She quickly noted down an address for Joe and they hugged once more before Mia closed the door. Her face was pained and having seen Sam it was evident that she was better at putting on a game face, sadly her Mum was the reality reminder and closing the door proved harder than she thought.

Sam waved as she pulled off the driveway and at

the same time, she hit the number she had for Jed and told him she would pick him up on route; he would be ready.

Driving through the darkened neighbourhood both Sam and Jed commented on the area with Jed saying he hoped he would never end up somewhere like that.

Sam agreed, adding that she hoped Grace hadn't either.

'What if we find her here?' he asked and for the first time in 6 months Sam tried to let that possibility sink in; what would she do if they found her? Trying to deal with the hurt and pain was something, but they could be faced with her granddaughter being right in front of them, scooping her up and returning her to her mother? Were they really dealing with her son-in-law being someone who could do this to his own daughter? Or her daughter?

Jed read out the street names as they twisted and turned around the darkened corners, eventually slowing down outside a block of flats.

'That one' pointed Jed. Sam pulled up and turned off the ignition. She then looked at Jed and he gestured a nod, told her to grab her jacket and to keep close, he could already see gangs hanging around.

'Let's not cause unnecessary attention' Sam

warned, with Jed smiling at her and saying he knew why they were there and she could rely on him to keep calm. This was the closest they had been to a new lead; he was not going to let that blind him.

Sam went slightly ahead when walking into the building, finding a couple making out in the foyer with no care they were on view.

Jed looked away first and caught Sam's elbow as he headed up the staircase with her, both hearts racing and at the top of the staircase Jed pointed once more, this time to the red door.

Jed looked over the bannister to see if the couple were still preoccupied and they were. He then placed his fore finger on his lips to signal silence and placed his ear to the door, but nothing.

He tried looking through the peep hole and although he felt sure he saw movement; he could not see or hear a child.

Sam said she was going to knock; Jed stood to the side.

After a light tap Joe's voice called out that he was coming and the door opened. His face was a picture; shock, surprise and then anger.

'*What are you doing here?*' he demanded. Sam stepped in front of Jed who received the same welcome and pretty much pushed her way in.

'*Grace? Grace?*' she called out frantically and

left Jed stunned that she had forgotten the line of questioning they had run through in the car. Joe looked around in panic.

'*What the fuck?*' he shouted and Jed noticed that his face flushed with colour; looking back at Jed, certainly more concerned that he was involved.

Sam checked the rooms but there was no evidence of Grace or of a child having stayed. '*Where is she?*' she screamed and with the full force of her body, she thumped his chest until he fell back against the wall.

'*Sam, you've fucking lost it*' he shouted but just as he went to force her off, Jed stepped forward and pulled her back.

'*Sam*' Jed insisted '*This is not helping!*'

Sam was spitting as she cried, tears flowing freely and Joe was still in shock, his hands raised in surrender. '*I don't get it*' he shouted.

'*Lower your voice*' threatened Jed. '*I'm going to close the door and we are going to talk ok?*' With that he stepped back and closed the door aware that the young couple were now half way up the staircase and this unnerved him. They were definitely being watched.

Sam walked away but continued to argue with herself, throwing expletives at Joe as she paced.

Jed pulled up a kitchen chair and ordered Joe to sit,

then he pulled another and sat opposite him, their knees touching. *'Are we going to expect someone to come barging in?'* he asked and Joe flashed a look to the door. *'No'* he whimpered.

Jed began with questions, not mentioning the fire escape, but focusing on the fact that Joe was now living here and why, asked him questions that would hopefully put him at ease and throw him off their real reason for dropping by.

Sam was now sitting in the armchair, her hands crossed in front of her face, willing herself to keep it together, not to interfere with Jed who was doing what he did best.

'What are you doing for money?' Jed asked and then looked around the room with it's damp walls and mouldy curtains. *'Why here?'* he continued.

Joe looked across to Sam, then he welled up and started trembling. *'Losing Grace was too much'* he spoke slowly. *'Mia would never forgive me; we couldn't get through it'*

'Forgive you for what?' Jed asked, focusing on his emotional weakness *'Why would she blame you?'* he adjusted his position.

'You hear about it all the time. Couples who go through terrible things and then break up, each blaming the other' Jed noticed Joe now grew stronger and his words firmer, fuelled with frustration. *'She should have been a better Mother!'* he exclaimed.

'Looked after her properly and then this wouldn't have happened!'

Sam rose to react but Jed raised his hand without looking at her and tapped Joe's thighs in front of him.

'Go on, I'm with you there' Jed carried on, much to Sam's frustration and pain. 'I have twins and God knows, I cannot deal with that all day long so I am happy to bring in the money but my wife … 'Jed drew breath and sat up straight 'My wife wants to return to work and '**share**' childcare, but Joe, I am with you …she wanted the kids!' Jed laughed as he spouted on 'That's the term **Mother,** eh? We fall out regularly as she wants to arrange childcare and I'm like, you are the mother!'

Joe started to nod 'That's it' he said and Sam watched as the two continued to berate women, finding a shared platform.

'I love them, don't get me wrong' Jed explained 'but I want them to have a Mum, right?' Joe nodded enthusiastically 'exactly'

Jed then raised up from his chair, walked away a couple of steps and returned abruptly to stare Joe in the face.

'The difference between us Joe is I would die for mine, I would absolutely die for them, kill anyone who ever laid a hand on them and if they tried to take them from me or my wife … well, that is the worst *thing I can think of …'*

Joe gulped and sat back, his hands now on his chest, ready to protect himself again.

'*So, why Joe?*' Jed leaned closer, his hands resting on Joe's chair, either side of his shoulders with their noses nearly touching.

'*As a parent, however pissed off you may be with the missus, you wouldn't, couldn't, do anything that would hurt your own child? I'm right, am I not?*'

Joe nodded, then whilst Jed held his position, he slowly opened his eyes to fix on Jed's glare. '*I …*' Joe couldn't speak clearly '*I … err*' Jed tilted his head

'*You what?*' he said, this time he pushed Joe's chair back slightly causing Joe to jolt, forcing him to grab Jed's arms.

'*You what?*' Jed repeated, deliberately mouthing the words slowly, slamming the chair back down onto the floor.

'*Stop, please, just stop*' Joe broke down, crying and pleading with Jed to stop and through his tears they could hear him apologise to Sam, then sobbing and calling out to Grace that he was sorry.

Sam went over to Joe and crouching down by his side she held his hand.

'*Joe, I don't care why, not now, but I do want to know where she is? I am begging you, please, please let us bring her home?*'

Joe put his hands over his face and cried like never before, again saying that Mia would never forgive him and that he couldn't forgive himself for what he had done.

Jed encouraged Sam to stand closer and with his body he stepped slightly in front of her as if he knew what would happen next.

'Joe' he spoke so calmly. *'Joe, look at me?'* Jed repeated.

Joe's face was wet with tears but slowly he raised his face and looked at Jed, still whimpering and biting his lip.

'Is Grace alive?'

Sam squealed and reeled back from the statement, with Jed managing to keep her back long enough for Joe to start blubbering once more.

'Is she?' he raised his voice again. *'Damn you Joe, you answer me quickly or I will kill you myself!'*

Joe came to an abrupt stop and gulped down his tears, swiping away snot from his lips.

'I don't know' he said *'I honestly don't know'* He then fell down onto his arms, crying at the table.

Jed looked behind to see Sam in a state of shock; touching her hand he tugged at her gently and asked her if she was with him. She nodded but could not speak.

'Sam, we need to get the facts, find out what happened and follow the trail ok ... you with me Sam? I need you? Grace needs you?'

Sam shook her head and pulled herself back to the room, barely unable to focus.

Jed pulled the chair so he faced Joe. 'Start talking' he demanded.

'Gracie should have been at home, with her Mum' he started but Jed kicked his shin and said he wasn't interested in hearing his parenting advice, he wanted to hear what happened on the day she was abducted 'because she was, wasn't she?' he repeated 'Abducted?'

Joe nodded but then corrected Jed 'No, she was with me?'

Sam couldn't help but butt in 'She was supposed to be with Sylvia, not you, you piece of shit!'

Jed gave Sam a glare, the not helpful one, she knew.

'We weren't getting on, fighting, arguing, the usual' Joe told them 'and Mia would not hear it that Grace was being neglected and that morning she told me the best thing I could do for both of them was leave ... leave, she said?!'

Jed gestured for him to continue 'go on' he said.

'I went to work, joke of a job, boss told me that I wouldn't get my bonus that month either. Fucking knob, said I hadn't put in the time? What was he talk-

ing about? I work 6 days a week, minimum 12-hour days, not putting in the time? That was it, I told him to stick it and left'

'What about Grace?' shouted Sam. Joe looked over at her, his eyes softer and begging for forgiveness.

'I drove for an hour or two, had a drink I think, then drove to get Grace' he paused and reflected for a moment before Jed nudged his leg to continue.

'I noticed the neighbour closing the door and going in your apartment?' he continued to watch Sam for an indication that she believed him.

'I'm her father, but neither of you even bothered to tell me she spends time with the neighbour!' his voice accusing. 'I was confused?' he continued. 'I was in a bad place ok, so by the time I got to the top of the stairs, rather than knocking on your door and getting Grace like I planned, I turned left and knocked on Rick's door …' Joe sighed heavily. 'He took one look at me and asked if I wanted to score?' Sam looked away; she couldn't bear to look at him any longer. Jed asked him if he had 'scored' before.

'Years ago,' said Joe. 'I knew of the guy, Sam had mentioned him a couple of times, you know, the drug dealer at the end of the hall?' he continued to look to Sam who turned the other way.

'He said he had seen me but didn't need any hassle, so to piss off' Joe sighed again 'But I didn't, *did I? Said I needed something and he could tell I was in a bad way and the moment I pulled out a wadge of cash he let me in.'*

'*So, you went in and got high?*' asked Jed. Nodding in agreement Joe went on to say that he wasn't there for long, or so he thought but it must have been an hour or more because when the Police asked him about entering the building, they were able to confirm the CCTV.

'*That's a good point*' remarked Jed '*How come you went in by the front door and we know you left by the fire escape, with Grace?*' he added.

Joe looked caught out as Jed continued '*But then you are seen leaving the apartment a little later, this time through the front, which is why you were eliminated?*'

'*Yeah, I told Rick about my life, about her mother and he said there was a lesson to be learned? He told me I should take her away for a few days, see how she feels when she can't see her for awhile and yeah, that seemed like a good idea at the time*'

Joe called over to Sam who was still unable to look at him.

'*Just to teach her a lesson Sam*' he said '*She would re-think her relationship with Grace and make changes. I promise you that was it!*'

Jed said to continue '*... so, what happened?*' he pushed.

'He said he would fix me up with something to take with me and to get Grace and come back to his, I could take her out via the fire escape so it would shit her up when they checked the CCTV' Joe chuckled. 'A dumb fuck like that, but he had it all worked out!' he continued. 'I went to the apartment' said Joe.

'Off your face!' spat Sam, before turning away promptly.

'Yeah, still off my face' Joe admitted 'I put the key in the door and as I pushed it open, I realised there was giggling and noises coming from the bedroom and my baby was alone on the sofa watching tv!' Joe lowered his head, looked genuinely hurt as he explained how he picked her up and she beamed, her little face so happy to see him.

The bedroom noises were building and he knew Sylvia shouldn't have a male visitor in the bedroom and certainly not to leave his daughter alone. He was outraged and once again Grace was being neglected! He scooped her up and left the apartment and before he had thought it through, he entered Rick's.

What he hadn't expected was the next stage of the plan 'Your plan?' Jed reminded him.

'No, I told you, I was going to take her away with me for a few days, show Mia what she was missing, that was it!' Joe pleaded. 'Then I get there and even her paid childminder was not minding her! I wasn't thinking straight ok, I know that, but Rick said *why don't you teach them all a lesson and it sounded like a good idea at the time, they didn't deserve her'.*

Joe stood up and Jed blocked him from passing. *'Joe, you need to tell us everything'*

Joe leant against the table, his heart heavy and face full of regret and remorse. *'He suggested we head down the fire escape, that would throw them off if they checked the CCTV he said. I didn't question it'*

Jed went to the sink and downed a glass of water, then raised his tone a little, as if he was clearing a path to the truth.

'Once at the bottom he persuaded me to put Grace in his car, which was parked in the alley and to head back up, stroll down the staircase and out the front door where I would be seen without her, 'perfect cover' he said and yeah, I wanted to mess with you all'

Sam spoke quietly when she reminded him that Grace was no pawn, she shouldn't have been used in a petty argument and Jed could do no more than agree.

'I will regret doing it for the rest of my life' he said.

'So, where did you take her?' asked Jed.

'Well, that's it' said Joe. *'I walked out of the building and the car was gone!'*

Sam rushed forward *'Gone? With a crackhead?'* she screamed. Jed held Sam firm.

'*Tell me Joe, tell me she's alright?*' begged Jed. '*Come on mate, up to that point, I see you were pissed off with women and you thought you'd teach them a lesson, but after that? Come on, you know where Rick lives, you could have told Sam or the Police? What the fuck?*'

Joe started coughing and struggled to get his breath. Jed wacked him hard on the back and eventually he gained control.

'*I got Jose to call him and she was pretty upset, though I think he had beaten her earlier that day, she was bruised and bleeding*' Joe raised his hands. '*I begged her to find out where they had taken Grace and to be fair to her, she called him a couple of times; that's when he asked for money*'. Joe sat down. '*Money*' he repeated with despair. '*I had lost my job that day, no money, my wife? … well, 'excuse me dear' I handed our daughter to a crackhead who is now demanding money if we ever want to see her again?*'

Jed made a guttural noise and both Sam and Joe stared at him. '*I told you earlier that I would die for mine, but you were worried for yourself … when you were faced with the impossible, you were worried for yourself?*'

Joe piped up '*You said you get it; your wife took the mick? didn't want to be a Mother*?'

'*I was lying to get you on side, you fucking low life!*' Jed barked.

Joe ran his fingers through his hair *'fuck, fuck'* he started to chant.

'When did you last see her?' Sam asked.

'That day' whimpered Joe *'That was the last day. The day I handed my daughter to a total stranger'*

Jed turned to Sam *'Let's go'* he grabbed his jacket and summoned Sam to follow.

'Wait, where are you going?' Joe called after them, the panic in his voice evident.

'Where do you think?' shouted Jed.

'No, hold on' cried Joe. *'There's more'*

Jed stopped, his hand on the open door and Sam a second behind him. He scowled, threatening Joe to speak now or he would be back, regardless of the fact that he was their only link to Grace right now.

Joe held out his hand, begging them to hear him out; *'Wait, please'* he pleaded to Jed. Again, his hands flailing in front. *'Close the door'* he begged.

Sam walked back to Joe; her voice wavered as she lowered herself to a crouching position near him.

'Joe, listen to me …' she started off gently. *'I need to know …'* now her voice was breaking and tears filled her eyes. *'Is she alive?'*

With that she lowered her head and tried to take control of her own breathing, swiping tears from her cheek, staring him straight in the eyes, her voice getting firmer *'Is she …?'*

Jed called out from the door that this was a waste of time and Sam told him to hold on.

'Joe?' Sam never looked away and Joe closed his eyes momentarily, then looked into Sam's with a cold determination. *'She has to be'* he murmured.

'Have you any proof?' Sam replied and with a breath that took her by surprise, he nodded as he cried, pulling out a photograph from his shirt pocket which Sam snatched immediately.

She dropped to the floor, her legs gave way beneath and trying to clear her blurry vision, she sniffled *'Oh my God, its recent!'* she called to Jed.

Jed let the door go and joined Sam on the floor, the two of them staring intently at the picture of little Gracie.

'It's definitely recent' she repeated and Jed looked a little shaken too, tears appearing in his eyes.

'Yeah, I can tell' he broke. *'Sam, I wasn't sure before, but now …?'*

Jed looked over Sam's shoulder and taking the photograph from Sam's damp fingers, he waved it in front of Joe, who was looking paler by the second.

'When was this?' he demanded, shaking it

harder before Sam retrieved it and once again stared closely at the little blonde in the picture.

'*When?*' he shouted '*Who gave it to you?*' Joe tried to adjust his seating position but Jed placed his hand on Joe's chest '*answer me!*'

'*Wait*' Sam tried to stand and Jed rose with her, looking down at Joe who tried to stand too, but Jed refused. '*Talk now or I swear ...*'

'*Jed, please, back off*' shouted Sam. '*This is the closest we have ever been, please, let me talk to him?*'

Jed walked about the room, with Sam perching next to Joe. '*You said there was more?*' her hand now on his thigh. '*What's happening? Who gave you the photo Joe? Please ... now is the time to tell us everything you know? This isn't about right or wrong, nothing can change the past and this is not the time for recrimination either. You want her back safe, don't you? You can help us?*'

Joe pushed himself up off the chair and rested against the breakfast bar, wiping his eyes and clearing his throat. He nodded profusely. '*I am doing everything I can and have done so ever since that day, I swear Sam*' he had his hands out trying to convey his frustration.

'*Every day I do what is asked of me, with the sole purpose of getting her back; I had to play along just to keep her safe, you can see why? I couldn't risk telling anyone and believe me if I thought it would have gone on this long, then I would have told the Police at the start but these people Sam ...'* Joe coughed a couple of times, crying as he tried to apologise over and over.

'Go on' Jed raised his voice from the other side of the room and again Sam gestured for him to wait and let Joe talk.

'The photo is one of a few, you know, as proof or I wouldn't do anything else for them' Sam nodded that she accepted that.

Joe looked over at Jed, who was pacing, then back at Sam and this time he put his hands either side of her shoulders and pulled her towards him.

'Listen Sam' Joe's words clear and firm. *'Now that you know, we can work together and get her back, can't we?'* he said but before Sam could reply he continued *'I don't care about me, my life is over, let's be honest ... but Gracie?'*

'Yes, exactly' Sam approved. *'What's the plan?'* she asked, her eyes wide with hope.

'Do you move drugs for him?' Joe nodded briefly then explained that he knows there is more to it than that, that he does pick up and move drugs of course, but there have been other times

'Yeah?' questioned Sam, her voice in a rush, but Joe started to breakdown at this point.

'God forgive me' he cried. *'What?'* Sam pulled back from his grip *'What Joe, tell me?'*

'*There are others*' he sobbed. Jed rushed from the other side of the room and pulled Joe away, shaking him furiously, then grabbing his face, he was nose to nose with Joe, their spit exchanged as Joe cried and Jed threatened to expose him then and there.

'*You slimy bastard*' he snarled and it took Sam a few minutes to release Joe from his grip; not before Jed took a swing at him, catching the corner of his eye.

'*Jed!*' shouted Sam, her body weight pushing him back as far as she could and thumping his chest, begging him not lose their only way ahead.

'*We can help them too*' she started to splutter and cry, pleading with Jed to back off. '*Jed please?*'

Jed lowered his head and placed his hands on his own thighs, taking in deep breaths trying to gain control of his anger.

'*Other families like yours Sam, all desperate to find their children?*' he pointed at Joe '*He could have let us in, informed the Police, but he's trying to save his own neck!*' he shouted.

Sam agreed, returned to Joe and pushed him against the wall

'*Enough now*' her tone controlled. '*Jed can get in doors, that I can't*' she told him. '*We will let Jed do what he can legally?*' Joe nodded, whimpering, snot running down his face, now mixed with a little blood from the cut above his eye.

'We can concentrate on Grace' Sam assured him and Joe continued nodding silently.

'Jed can feed info back and maybe we can turn this situation around for a few families eh?' Sam smiled and tried to encourage Joe to trust them and tell them what they needed to know.

The next half hour was fraught but finally Sam could see a pattern emerging and so much more made sense, all the time she was thinking perhaps tomorrow would be the day; the day she took her granddaughter home ... Mia? What would she say to Mia?

She shook her head, tried to lose that train of thought; not something she needed to resolve at the today.

'I need you to come back to my place' Sam told Joe; aware Jed was not in agreement with that to begin with.

'I have a timeline I need you to look at?' she explained. *'I have a few photos too ...'* she lowered her stare to look into Joe's tearstained face *'This is how you put things right Joe*?' Joe nodded his heavy head and was relieved to share the burden of his plight with Sam, to share the pain with someone who loved his little girl.

As they walked out of the building the couple that had been hanging around the staircase gave Joe a look, he told them he was fine and would be back. Neither Sam or Jed reacted or spoke to Joe as they left the building but walking over to the car, they were acutely aware they were being followed.

Joe started to walk towards the back seat but Jed gestured to Joe to get in the passenger seat, which he did and Jed climbed in the back. He hoped that this would look as though Joe was not leaving against his will and to help out Joe raised his hand to the couple as the car pulled away.

'*Keep talking*' Jed said and pulled himself forward, his warm breath on Joe's neck.

'*Do you know where she is at the moment?*' he asked but Joe shook his head.

'*No, within the first few days, they took me to see her so of course I returned late one night and got jumped; Grace had been moved*' Joe ran his sweaty fingers through his hair and sighed deeply.

'*After that I couldn't locate her, so when I said I wouldn't do anything else until I saw her, they let me have a photograph*'

Sam was driving a little faster now and Jed suggested she slow it down as they neared her apartment, her eyes drawn to the side of the building's fire escape.

She stopped the car and turned to Joe.

'*That day*' she started '*When you came down and the car was gone?*' Joe exhaled deeply.

'*The day my heart was stolen*' he added. '*You were high, right?*' Joe confirmed he was, but said he sobered up pretty quickly.

'*How did you hear from Rick?*' Sam questioned but Jed tapped Joe on the shoulder and beckoned Sam to get out of the car and head inside.

As they entered the foyer, Sam placed her finger on her lips and pointed ahead for Joe to go first. She didn't want to talk in the open but by the time they got to the top of the stairs, the door at the end of the corridor opened slightly and they were aware they were being watched.

Once inside Jed stood by the door and sure enough Sally shuffled along, unable to rise up on tip toe and look through the peep hole but Jed could see the top of her head as she rested her ear to the other side of the door.

He pulled it open with a jolt and Sally stumbled forward. '*Can I help you with something?*' he snapped.

Sally adjusted her clothing and tutted at him '*I was just walking past*' she grumbled '*You opened the door too quick ... it pulled me in!*'

With that Sally returned to her apartment and Jed started to close the door but not before noticing a familiar figure climbing the stairs towards him.

No words were spoken, just a lingering look as Rick continued by, smirking before turning towards his own apartment.

Jed wasn't sure whether Joe had been seen entering Sam's apartment but Jed was aware it could cause Rick to act dangerously if he thought they were on to him so Jed stepped inside and closed the door. This time he stood close to the door until he heard Rick's apartment door slam shut.

Joe was studying the wall, his hands running through his greasy hair and then covering his mouth, tears of despair once again running down his face.

Sam placed her hand on Joe's shoulder and found herself momentarily feeling empathy for her son-in-law.

She whispered close to his ear that it was time for action, now more than ever and that 6 months was too long for Grace to be away from home and Joe nodded as he swiped thick mucus from his nose.

Sam offered a tissue, then walking behind him she pointed to the man in the van.

'*Do you recognise him?*' she asked. Joe was shaking his head

'*No, why?*' he turned to her. '*Who is he?*'

Sam sighed and rested her body on the arm of the sofa '*I was praying you would be able to tell me?*' she said. '*What about Sir Geoffrey?*' she continued hopefully, but again Joe shook his head and once more ran his wet hands through his unkempt hair.

'Sam' his voice raised slightly 'What do you know? What do you know about any of it?' he pleaded. 'This is your world isn't it?' and with that he turned around completely to face her, his arms outstretched, desperate.

'The one thing that kept me going was that even though I let this happen, Grace had the best grandmother ... I mean, who else knew how this worked? You dig up everyone's dirt, you investigate so many things, every day?' Joe was looking over at Jed, then back to Sam for confirmation.

Sam again sighed heavily, then looking up at Joe spoke with a low growl 'You did this Joe' she said '... and just to be clear, this isn't something that we deal with every day. We are an Agency, who search for people, yes, but we have to pass on to the Police any information that crosses over to the illegal, where we need enforcement.

Every situation is different, some missing people come home by themselves but children? That's something the Police deal with ... some are trafficked, some are held hostage or ransomed, so you tell me Joe, which one would our little girl be in danger of? Hey?' Sam stood up straight and pushed Joe, causing him to stumble.

Jed hurried over and pulled Sam by her arm, reminding her that they needed to work together, not against each other, then Joe's mobile rang.

Joe pulled out his phone and with a panic across

his face mouthed *'It's Rick!'* Sam and Joe stared at each other.

'Answer it' Jed ordered *'But don't lie, he may have seen you come in'* he added.

Colour drained from Joe's face but Jed pushed the mobile closer and once more ordered Joe to answer.

'Answer the bloody thing' he said. *'it wouldn't be odd for you to be here you idiot, answer it!'*

Joe raised the phone to his ear and spoke and they were able to hear Rick's voice on the other end, Joe unable to take his gaze away from Jed's, in hope of direction.

'What you up to?' Rick asked. Joe coughed to clear his throat and shrugged his shoulders before Jed gestured, he should continue.

'I er … I'm just at my mother-in-law's place' he said and then there was silence. Once more Joe shrugged his shoulders but Sam gestured to him to stay quiet, until eventually Rick spoke.

'Down the corridor eh?' he asked.

'Yeah' said Joe. *'What can I do for you?'* he asked as he began to move.

'It'll keep' said Rick. *'Call me when you're free'* he demanded, before ending the call.

Joe threw the mobile onto the sofa, then lowering his head he placed his hands on his thighs and tried to control his breathing.

Jed picked up the phone and began scrolling through while Sam rose up from the arm of the sofa and went over to Joe.

'You'll be able to tell him something that works' she said. 'I mean to keep up appearances, you would be dropping by, wouldn't you, asking if there was any news?' she said and Joe looked up, knowing what she was suggesting was plausible

'Yeah, true … we would be supporting each other, right?' he agreed.

Jed stopped at a few numbers and transferred information over to his own mobile before asking Joe to confirm some names.

'When he calls like that' Jed started 'What happens after?' Jed dropped down into the armchair closer to Joe, pointing to the one opposite and suggesting he take a seat.

Joe rested back in the chair, his eyes closed momentarily and his chest still rising fully as he inhaled and exhaled slowly. He nodded, then leant forward towards Jed.

'He told me yesterday to be available today so this will piss him off' Joe explained.

'What's happening today? Joe put out his hands 'No idea … not yet anyway' he said. 'I get told when he calls, then I do whatever'

Joe looked to Sam and his voice changed tone *'Does Mia have any idea about my involvement?'* he asked, nervously. Sam stared at him, enough to force him to turn away in shame.

'How could I tell her anything?' she said. *'She told me you two were separated but not for one second do I think she knows that Grace's father could have done this!'* she snapped.

'That is a conversation to have with her another day and I pray for all our sakes that it is after she has Grace back in her arms' Sam was close enough now to hit his shoulder. *'You hear me?'* she barked and Joe nodded, relieved that he could prolong that a little longer.

Jed listened to a couple of voicemails on Joe's phone, then holding the mobile away from his ear so they all could hear, he asked Joe who the gravelly voice belonged to but Joe shrugged his shoulders again, desperate for answers himself.

'No idea' he replied. *'I only know that on that day I had to meet him in Leicester Square and collect a package for Rick. Rick met me at the tube station and then … that was it'.* He looked about vaguely before continuing *'I mean, that's it so far where drugs are concerned'*

'Definitely drugs?' asked Jed. Joe nodded *'Yeah, definitely drugs when that happens and every time I am just waiting for a hand on my shoulder or a bust of some sort with me framed right in the middle*

and to be honest I have wished that so many times, just to tell the Police my side, to shed light on all of the twisted bastards that are involved in this and well, I don't know, but maybe by telling everyone it will bring out the big guns?'

'*Then you think of Grace?'* suggested Sam, her face tilted to the side as Joe looked over his shoulder.

'*Then I think if I just do this one more time … maybe tomorrow I get her back?'*

It was clear to see that Joe had got drawn into something too big to get out of, but as to how they handle the situation moving forward, well that was proving more complicated by the hour.

'*Now what?'* Sam asked Jed. Jed was sitting back in his chair, looking at Joe who was lost, emotionally wrecked and lost.

'*We are going to send you home Joe, whether you go to Rick's door now on your way out, or go outside and call him to say you are free, but didn't want to be seen by us by heading down the corridor, I don't know … either way, you better see what he wants and we will be in touch with you, or you with us?'*

Joe agreed, his legs shaking as he stood, turning one last time to look at Sam who found herself losing sight of a lead, the enthusiasm they had been riding these past 48 hours had brought them here; the thought of Joe or Rick being their way forward was altogether terrifying.

Closing the door behind Joe, Sam cried.

'Hey, don't lose momentum' he whispered but all she could do was cry.

It was agreed Jed would head on home and Sam thanked him for his help. He was due back in the office tomorrow and she knew how much strain this would be putting on him, his workload and even his home life, though Lisa had been nothing but supportive.

As Sam locked the door behind him, she realised she hadn't even managed to eat something but now hunger raised its head.

The kettle whistled and Sam dropped a tea bag into the large cup in front of her. She slowly ran her thumb over the words *'Nana'* as she held back more tears and forced herself to remain calm; then the door knocked.

'Who is it?' Sam called out. *'Jamie'* came a gruff reply. Sam quickly placed her eye to the peep hole, then a moment of panic took hold as she glanced across the room.

Opening the door slowly Sam adjusted her clothes and pushed back her hair, then offered a smile, still keeping her body in the space between them.

'Not going to invite me in?' he asked.

Unwillingly Sam stood aside, allowing the

Agency's Chief to enter and as he walked past, she raised her eyes to the ceiling, wishing she could have refused, followed by relief that Jed had left, just in time.

This 6ft 6in brute of a man, Naval ex-marine, had been an amazing mentor for Sam over the years and in turn Sam had become a very trusted and well-respected colleague and friend.

It was rare for Jamie to talk about his past, the places he had been or the sights he had seen, but needless to say, it had affected him deeply. There were obvious moments where the team could feel his need to pause, reflect, then with a small clearing of the throat he would remind them they had a job to do and head back to his office.

When an opportunity arose to help a friend, Jamie was first to offer and on leaving the military he found himself with no direction and suddenly his 'special skills' were no longer required. Quite what they were, was hard to define but he was quickly known as to the man to call if you needed to find someone, or to put pressure on someone?

The Agency came about because Jamie was offered a cash sum to investigate a small business, posing as a cover for drugs; information was to be gained before the Police were given the go ahead. It was a personal vendetta, an ex-employee with a gripe, but it gave him a purpose and some cash and that started his relationship with the Agency.

When the offices on the 2nd floor became available the Superintendent on the floor above suggested he consider being a private eye but a week later he was helping finding a missing person and so the Agency was born.

The Police were happy to have him alongside, offering their support and in turn the Missing Persons Agency could assist with groundwork and following possible leads. It was a great partnership.

Jamie always prided himself on being able to get the job done! He joked he was a better-looking Idris Elba, though it was agreed in the office there could only ever be one Idris!

'Jamie' Sam sighed as she closed the door.

'How are you doing?' he asked, his deep tone soothing.

Sadly, nerves were taking over and her voice warbled, still unable to look at him directly. Sam made her way back to the steaming cup of tea and offered him to join her; which he did.

Silence befell the room and caused Sam to turn round, then a knot in her stomach as she saw him studying the wall.

Slowly she walked over with his tea and placed it down on the table behind him.

'Listen' she sounded exasperated. Jamie looked down, his huge body shadowing hers.

'I am not here to judge you Sam' he said, then placed himself in the seat opposite.

'Ok' said Sam reassured. *'Is this official?'* she asked.

Jamie took a sip of tea, then placed the mug down.

'We all know how hard this must be for you Sam, no-one's taking that away from you, so let me make that abundantly clear'

'But?' Sam jumped in.

'But ...' continued Jamie *'There's talk ok'* Sam shook her head

'Wow' she said. *'I've left, what more do you want? My resignation? Then that's ok too, I'll do it right now but don't come to my home and tell me you understand what I'm dealing with and by the way stop making waves ... or what?'*

Jamie started to smile *'You've always been a fire-cracker Sam'* he smirked. *'Let me finish please, then you can berate me'* He raised his eyes wide *'Deal?'* he joked.

Sam lifted her tea to her lips in the hope it would stop her from speaking out while he explained.

'You know why you had to leave' he started. *'We need 100% Sam, we owe it to the clients we deal with and it was impossible for you to do that, so there was no other way. But we can't stop you continuing to search yourself and the Police are doing everything*

they can I know, plus your colleagues in the Unit, we are all doing what we can'

As he spoke, he removed his jacket and placed it over the arm of the chair before taking another sip of tea and continuing.

'I'm aware it's 6 months' he said, his voice gentle and emphatic *'Sam, you have been the heart of the Agency and no doubt to your family and yes, I do get to hear things ... you knew it would get back to me surely?'*

Sam wondered whether to answer straight away but then the words slipped out on their own *'Jed?'* she heard herself utter.

Jamie nodded *'Yes, Jed'* he confirmed. *'I know how close you are and you know we split you up as a team awhile ago, two reasons really; one that he is equal to you in his capability to head up a team and yes, a little bit of me felt you were too close to be objective at times, always looking to support each other and maybe not following your own instincts out of loyalty to the each other'*

Before he could continue Sam placed her cup down abruptly. *'Well, that doesn't make a lot of sense!'* she blurted out. *'We work off each other, not against each other, as you say, it's not like we push aside our gut instincts for want of hurting each other's feelings? That's ridiculous!'* she snapped.

Jamie again smiled *'I knew that would push a button*

but maybe from my position you would see it differently, see that I could have 2 as opposed to 1?'

Sam shook her head in frustration *'So?'* she raised her eyebrows. *'What now?'* she asked. Jamie had always liked her straight talking so he took a final gulp of tea and raised himself up from the chair, Sam following his lead.

He walked to the wall, his hands in his trouser pockets as he rocked backwards onto his heels. *'Impressive'* he said, then looked at the photographs, a little closer.

'Where are we now?' he asked and to her surprise she walked him through recent findings, ensuring him Jed had only been helping in his own time and that what he had managed to uncover in these past 48 hours showed exactly what they were capable of when they worked together.

Jamie looked down at her small frame once more, smiled and agreed. *'I came to tell you that if you need him, he's yours'* he looked smug.

Sam looked awkward for a moment, her face tilted, expression confused. *'You mean ...?'* she stopped mid-sentence but Jamie smiled broadly.

'I mean, he's yours full time Sam and I have organised his team and his remaining cases so there's no need to take that guilt on either'

Sam placed her hands over her mouth so as to not speak out of place, but the tears fell from her eyes and ran over tightly gripped fingers, she gulped as she tried to gain control but Jamie took hold of her hands and pulled them away, still clasping them tightly inside his own.

'*One more thing*' Jamie said and Sam held her breath and her tears to look up at him once more. Jamie let go of her hands and passed her a tissue, then explained why he had come to the decision and Sam nodded enthusiastically as he offered her more help than she could ever have hoped for.

'*Of course,*' Sam agreed '*Whatever I can do …*' Sam paused as she remembered for a moment that she was not officially working for the Agency at the moment.

'*It needs to stay that way for me, a little off the record I guess and I can't believe it has come to that, but there's an urgency for this to be resolved; for us all. You know this is a Police matter and therefore the Agency should not be involved?*'

'*Does Jed know*?' Sam asked. '*He will do when you tell him* 'Smiled Jamie and with that he replaced his jacket. '*He can keep me updated, ok?*'

Sam promised he would and with his guidance they could work out the best way to move forward without bringing too much attention to their involvement.

'*Don't lose faith*?' Jamie placed his hand on Sam's shoulders and smiled kindly as she returned the same and with the softest voice, she whispered 'thank you'.

As Jamie left the apartment and headed down the stairs, Sam was quick to close and lock the door behind him and rushed for her mobile to update Jed.

The two laughed aloud, recalling how difficult he had been in the past and even though Sam had agreed to assist '*off the record*', she was happy to have Jed by her side officially; sleep would be a welcome friend again tonight.

Day 3 - Friday

Sam woke early Friday morning and for the first time in a very long time she felt energized and buzzing. Feeling full of renewed confidence; not alone anymore, knowing she had the support, albeit on the quiet, of the Agency and its resources and contacts and that Jed could go between the two.

She looked over at the small picture frame sitting on her dressing table, Grace's smiling face looking back at her; today was a painful reminder that another month had passed yet Sam leapt out of bed, got dressed and was nearly out the door when she received a call from Joe.

He explained Rick's instructions were to head to Leicester Square and no doubt drugs were involved. He told Sam he would be in touch during the afternoon, but felt sure Rick had not suspected anything.

No sooner than Sam had pulled the door behind her, she received a message from Jed to say he was outside.

She didn't acknowledge Sally at the end of the corridor or a noise to the other side of her; just rushed down the stairs as quickly as she could and headed out onto the street.

Jed pulled up and they sped off, both beaming that

they had been given the opportunity of working together again, that Grace had a real chance of being found faster and it wasn't lost on them that their expertise was being denied to other families, while searching for their own. Oh, please God let her be alive.

Sam updated Jed and where they initially wondered about a tail for Joe, Sam was desperate not to raise suspicion, at any cost; there were too many loose ends at the moment and so much promise had been gained from the last 2 days, it begged the question, what would they uncover today?

Jed drove through the city, knowing it well and finally pulled up at the Agency gates, he asked Sam to wait in the car whilst he nipped to the office.

When he returned, he was clasping paperwork, coupled with a confident smile. Sam tried to focus on staying positive but this new opportunity brought a vulnerability and an emotional connection now she could let Jed in. She wanted so much to be a support and strength to him too so it was important to keep it together.

'*Hold this*' he chirped as he passed her the file. Then turning the key, he pulled the car out of the layby and drove on through the busy streets.

'*What is it?*' asked Sam as she fingered the pages, then her expression changed to one of surprise and dismay

'*Really*?' she asked and Jed laughed aloud, '*Oh yeah baby!*'

He had called Jamie after speaking with Sam the evening before and after his initial thanks he had requested a few things himself. He had been advised to come in first thing and to sign off with his team and whilst there Jamie handed him a file that he believed to be useful.

It held names and contacts for so many, that both Sam and Jed would have used in the past and suddenly networks opened up for them but they had to move with caution as the Police had already been privy to these and if they realised the Agency were getting in the way, it could put a stop to everyone.

Sam clasped the file to her chest and momentarily closed her eyes; this was unheard of, though she remained aware there was more to this than being given Jed's support.

Jed drove them to his home where Lisa welcomed them and after an initial conversation with Sam, left them to it. Jed spread paperwork on the dining room table.

Between the two, many calls were made and some were positive, no main leads but it was surprising how information generates questions and Jed felt particularly confident that he would hear back from a couple of his regulars.

'*Look here*' Sam slid a piece of paper across to Jed who in turn pulled it close, then looked up at Sam.

'*Frosty?*' he said, then a snarled lip appeared.

'*Yes, but read underneath*' Sam pointed.

Jed read a small paragraph which connected Frosty to money laundering, something neither of them had known about in the past.

'*When was that?*' he asked but Sam couldn't confirm. Then she sat back and thought for a moment

'*Is that why he became a narc?*' she suggested. '*To keep him out of prison, because he couldn't be linked with the other?*'

Jed looked puzzled himself but then said it was a conversation to have with Frosty and Sam reminded him to watch his temper; adding it was no help '*to make waves*'

The morning flew by but the pair felt energised and proactive knowing they had officially been given the support they needed.

Sam's phone rang and Joe's name appeared on screen. '*Put him on loud speaker*' suggested Jed.

Sam touched the answer button, then tapped the speaker as she was placing it down on the table. That second of not speaking proved to be invaluable as a different voice entered the room.

'*Sam*?' he said. '*I know you can hear me*' he continued. Sam and Jed froze, their eyes locked, Jed pressing his finger to his lip, then his hand circled in the air telling Sam to answer.

'*Who's this*?' she asked. '*Why do you have Joe's phone?*'

'*I wanted to hear your voice*' he continued.

'*Well … hello*' Sam answered, her hands clasped in front of her and her heart beating faster. '*But I don't know who you are? Are you a friend of Joe's??*'

His heavy breath could be heard down the phone, raw and gruff. '*Joe's not able to talk right now*' he went on to say '*He's been a silly boy actually*' said the voice.

'*What does that mean*?' asked Sam. '*Put him on the phone please*?' But the voice gave a short laugh, then cleared his throat before saying Joe would be back later and hopefully, he would realise how lucky he was to get a second chance.

Before Sam could say anything else, the phone went dead and Sam clasped her hands over her mouth and gasped.

'*No, no …*' she cried. '*What has he done?*' Jed sat back.

'*Fuck!*' he gasped. '*If he's mentioned us? … Let's go to yours, Joe will head there*'

Their return journey was even faster with Jed nipping in and out side streets and overtaking unnecessarily, his foot heavy on the pedal.

'Slow' pleaded Sam. *'In one piece please?'*

Once inside the apartment, Sam paced the floor, regularly glancing at her phone for an answer.

'Perhaps I should ring him?' she suggested, but Jed advised her to wait.

An hour later Joe arrived at the door and Sam was quick to bustle him inside, his face was bruised and he had cuts to his lip and above his eye; he was in great pain, holding his ribs.

'What did you do?' Sam squealed.

Joe was bent double and tried to lower himself onto the sofa; Jed threw him a tea towel which he placed against his bloody lip.

Holding out his hand to stop Sam, Joe tried to speak and eventually Jed intervened.

With a mumble and occasional squint from discomfort, Joe attempted to explain.

He had arrived at the usual place to collect the package but this time he was met by a different man; a man he hadn't seen before, so initially he was unsure about a handover.

The guy got pretty frustrated and Joe wondered if he was wired? Was he Police? As he wasn't sure he turned to walk away saying he thought he had the wrong guy but as he started to leave, he was aware of a sharp pain in his back so he stopped and was escorted to a nearby bench where he was told not to move.

'*Go on*' encouraged Sam '*What did you do that pissed him off? Why did he take your phone?*' she snapped.

Again, Jed asked her to ease up and told Joe to spit it out; to tell them everything.

'*He pulled my phone from my hand*' Joe started to well up.

'*Keep talking!*' demanded Sam so Joe cleared his throat and tried again. '*He started to look through my phone and on the screen there's a picture of Gracie and I swear Sam, when he looked at her face ….*'. Joe paused, shook his head and aggression flooded his face

'*I nearly lost it*' Joe started to shake his head furiously, wincing as his ribs hurt. '*He knew something, I fucking know it, so I said … you've seen her, haven't you?*'

Sam leaned forward '*What did he say?*' Joe sat back and pushed the tea towel under his shirt to pressure the wound.

'*He pushed the knife harder, it cut me, but I stared him straight in the eye and said all I wanted was to know if my daughter was alive?*'

Jed made his way to sit closer to Joe and asked

Sam to get him some water, then tried a gentler approach.

'*Listen mate, you're dealing with this shit every day, I get it, but it's important ... anything, everything, tell us?*'

'*He started scrolling through messages and must have found one from you, started getting all flustered saying I was talking with cops but it's because it says 'Agency', that's all*'

Sam rose sharply. '*Why the fuck does it say Agency?*' she shouted. Joe panicked at the ferocity of her voice.

'*Wait, wait ... I know three Sam's ok, so I named you Sam, in brackets (Agency)*'

Joe wiped his mouth once more '*He read some messages and then said let's give her a ring, shall we?*'

Jed tapped Joe's knee '*Ok, okay, so?*' Joe was still watching Sam strutting around but finally he turned to face Jed.

'*He thought I was talking to the Police I reckon? I don't know, but he wanted to scare me and unsettle you, maybe just to see who answered? I told him you were her grandmother, but he didn't believe me, so he called?*'

Joe tried to stand and with Jed's assistance, supported himself on the breakfast bar, close to the door.

'*You shouldn't have come here*' said Sam '*You were probably followed!*'

'*I had to risk that*' Joe explained. '*I needed to check something*' and with that he walked over to the timeline wall; Jed and Sam following behind.

'*Yeah*' said Joe as he pointed to the guy they previously named '*Ghost*' standing by the van. '*I had to be sure*' continued Joe '*but yeah, that's him*'

Sam pushed hair from her face '*We were doing better Jed, now we could lose her*' Jed began speaking slowly and quietly '*Come on, I need you to stay strong*' he continued '*Joe's identified the guy, so he is involved after all?*'

Joe's phone started to ring and Joe immediately dropped it on the sofa, gasping and stepping back. Rick's name was flashing on the screen.

'*Answer it*' demanded Jed but Joe shook his head fiercely, refusing to pick it up.

'*Now!*' demanded Jed and with that he grabbed the mobile and forced it into Joe's hand.

Joe was still shaking his head and begged Sam to answer it for him but Sam stood motionless and unable to speak, looking for Jed's guidance. Jed leaned forward and with a low growl he threatened Joe.

'*Answer it or I will offer you up myself and you will never see Grace again!*'

Joe put the phone to his ear and spoke, but for a moment there was silence.

'*Rick*?' he said. Again, silence and finally Rick could be heard asking Joe where he was. Jed quickly looked into Joe's face and signalled him to say that he was just next door, in Sam's apartment and although Joe looked confused, he nodded and told Rick exactly that.

'*What's going on*?' he asked and Joe shrugged his shoulders, his body fidgeting back and forth, his voice sounding nervous so Jed waved his hand in front of him, gesturing for him to slow down.

Joe took stock of his breathing and again followed Jed's instruction. '*All good*' he said.

'*Good*?' repeated Rick. '*When you're done there, we'll meet*' he continued. '*Call me when you're outside … and Joe?*' Joe blinked hard, his eyes now wide and alert.

'*Yeah*?' said Joe. Rick sighed heavily '*You better not be playing me?*' Joe coughed nervously to clear his throat '*Mate, I'm not*' he whispered. '*I'll call you later*' and with that the call ended. Joe threw the phone down once more and sat back on the chair, sweat falling from his face, his hair damp from perspiration. '*I'm a dead man*' he chanted, his head in his hands.

Jed paced the room '*Ok, okay, let's think this through*' he said aloud. '*So, you were expecting to do a handover but this guy ... the ghost guy, showed up, right?'* Joe was shaking his head vehemently, unable to speak.

Jed bent forward and snapped his fingers in front of Joe's face and bring him back to the conversation and situation at hand. *'Yeah, yes ... never met him before'* Joe confirmed.

'Did you do the drop?' Jed asked and again Joe shook his head *'Yeah, he had fucking knife!'*

Jed began pacing once more whilst Sam took to the armchair and wrapped her arms around her knees, tears free flowing, desperation visible for them both to see.

'So, whether he called Rick or not, he has the goods and Rick knows ... what? That you nearly gave him trouble? That he checked your phone and saw 'Agency'? ... which of course you know is for Sam and Rick will know she works for the Agency? Can't believe he wouldn't have checked her out?'

Joe sat upright, a moment of relief in his voice *'Yeah, you're right!'* he said. *'I think he did know that'* he continued. *'So, I did what I was asked to do, handed it over and leave, right?'*

'Was he the right guy though?' suggested Sam. The two men both flashed her a look but Sam repeated the statement.

'What if you speak with Rick and it was the wrong guy?'

Joe panicked and leapt up from his seat *'Shit!'* he blurted out. *'What if Sam's right?'* he grabbed Jed's shirt.

'What if I've fucked up?' Jed pushed Joe away and by doing so forced him to let go of his clothing.

'Look at the guy' Jed told them and pointed to the ghost figure on the photograph.

'He is the one we are looking for? I bet my life on it'

Joe was quiet, then followed with a lower tone to his voice, staring out the window.

'But it's not your life we're betting on, is it? it's mine' he said.

Sam rose from the chair sharply and before she could pass Jed to get to Joe, she spat out the words *'No, it's Grace's life, you prick!'*

Continuing to hold Sam back Jed pointed to the door and told Joe to make a move, to head outside before calling Rick. If he wanted him to come to the apartment then perhaps, he could head up the escape later but it didn't sit right for him to make his way to Rick's straight away.

Joe pulled the door behind him and Jed gently shook Sam's shoulders and tried to snap her out of it.

'Sam' he said and eventually Sam looked up. *'This all seems like a set back but believe me, it's not'* he told her. *'Think about it, we now know that this*

guy knows Rick? It all ties in and he's connected with Sir Geoffrey's brother, right?' Sam glanced towards the wall, then nodded, without uttering a word.

Jed released Sam from his grip and walked closer to the wall.

'Can't believe I am about to say this' started Jed *'But perhaps I need to talk to Frosty?'*

Sam agreed.

'He has been so helpful with getting together the time line and the photographs' Sam tried to point out. *'I mean, he has nothing to gain here Jed?'*

Jed smiled at Sam. *'I'll do it for you'* he said. *'Make a deal with the devil? That's what you want, right?'*

Sam offered a brief smile, acknowledging her statement. *'Yes'* she said. *'I'll pay the price'*

Sam picked up Jed's jacket and held it out to him. *'Go home to your family Jed'* she smiled, this time warm and reassuring, yet absolute exhaustion came with every sigh.

'I will contact Frosty and we could see him to-morrow, first thing?' she suggested and with that Jed gave Sam a salute and a wink and left the apartment.

For a moment Sam thought about texting Joe and asking him to let her know how he got on with Rick, but then corrected herself, realising the foolishness of her thoughts.

Day 4 - Saturday

The next morning felt like the total opposite to the day before.

Sam felt beaten and looking at Grace's photograph caused an intake of breath, a realisation that another night had passed. That this innocent child had been away from her family, scared and alone for another night ... where the hell was she? Not ever did Sam think she would wish her granddaughter was with a loving childless couple; caring for her dearly but she found herself visualising her running into their room, her favourite doll clasped in her chubby little hands. She pictured them greeting her with laughter and cuddles; at that precise moment, she prayed for it to be true.

A text message brought Sam back to the stark reality and it was from Jed saying he would be there within the hour to pick her up.

The evening before Sam had got a message to Frosty and he agreed to meet them first thing; adding that if Jed got *'heavy handed'* he would leave. Sam promised Jed would be kept at arm's length and reminded Frosty that he was only safe, so long as he continued to do the right thing.

Running the shower, Sam saw another missed call from Mia. She had spoken with her briefly a few days before when she was looking for Joe but there was no positive news to share with her, without divulging Joe's real involvement and that was an unbearable thought right now.

Being a weekend, Mia would be off work and closing her eyes whilst the steaming water ran over her sore eyes and tender skin, Sam wondered how Mia could stand the pain of living in the house where Grace lived, loved and played. The silence in her home must be deafening and Sam couldn't face questions this morning. She decided to ignore the call, allowing voicemail to take a message and instead concentrated on getting dried and dressed and heading out the door.

As Sam made her way down the stairs, she was aware Rick's door had opened but she was already down the first level when she heard a familiar voice call out.

'*In a rush*?' he jibed. Sam stopped and looked back to see Rick leaning over the banister above.

'*It's a Saturday*' he quipped. '*You work Saturdays too*?' he snarled.

Sam felt her blood run cold as she knew that this low life was an instigator in her granddaughter's abduction but with every part of her being, she found a small smile and forced a reply to leave her lips.

'*No rest for the wicked*' she replied, then before she could be asked further questions, she continued making her way down the stairs and through the foyer; finally, the noise from the street drowned him out.

Her stomach was churning and she could hardly make sounds out from feeling light headed but thankfully her reliable partner pulled up close to the kerb. Seconds later, they sped away.

Sam run through her conversation with Frosty the previous night and occasionally Jed would grunt or make a snide remark to which Sam corrected him instantly and took opportunities to remind him that it was imperative he got on board and quick! He, of course, promised to keep it together and knew the importance of their meeting.

As they pulled up outside the café and Jed parked the car, they could just make out Frosty sitting alone near the back, but enough shadow gave him cover.

'*Please?*' she whispered to Jed and he whispered back. '*Best behaviour, I promise*'

Upon entering the café, they were addressed by a waitress who explained there was a 15-minute wait for breakfast but Jed raised his hand and said no problem. The two made their way to the back of the room and Frosty stood up to acknowledge Sam, a second before he nervously acknowledged Jed, then lowered his eyes and sat back down.

The waitress appeared by Jed's side and poured out

2 more coffees, offering to take a food order if they wanted but reminding them once again there was a wait.

'*Coffee's fine*' replied Sam but Jed asked if it was possible to just have some toast and the waitress returned with a full plate.

'*Thank you for meeting us*' Sam told Frosty and although he didn't answer, he sipped his tea and his eyes flickered back and forth between them.

Jed cleared his throat after taking a bite of hot buttered toast and mouthful of coffee.

'*Yeah*' he agreed '*We appreciate your help*'

Sam took a deep breath and whilst the café gave way to noise, she pushed the photograph of the ghost towards Frosty and asked him if he remembered the picture?

Frosty again nodded but this time looked a little confused.

'*You were going to do some digging and get back to me?*' Sam continued.

Frosty put his cup down, then with a frown he started to mumble, spit spraying from his mouth. '*I told you all I knew*?' he started. His voice gravelly; his chest full of phlegm when he coughed, the result of decades of smoking and drug abuse.

Jed glanced to Sam, then back to Frosty. '*What does

that mean?' he asked but he leaned forward on the table and his hand slapped down a little bit firmer than he had meant to, causing Frosty to withdraw.

'*Sorry*' Jed offered. '*Didn't mean to demand, but we were waiting to find out about this guy? What do you know about him?*'

Sam was keen to keep things calm so she reiterated her confusion and reminded Frosty that he had given her the photo and said he was one to watch; that he had promised to get back to her?

Frosty took another gulp of tea, then wiped his wet mouth on his cuff, before coughing ferociously and finally spitting into a napkin.

'*Told your boss about him*' Frosty stared, his arms stretched out in wonder that they didn't know.

'*Our boss?*' questioned Sam.

'*Yeah, the big guy*' Frosty continued. '*He asked me to come in and I thought it was to see you, but he said you had been laid off or something …* '. Sam corrected Frosty briefly but this went over his head and he coughed again and once more continued. '*Yeah, well, he said I could tell him as he didn't know who would be taking over?*'

Sam closed her eyes and took a further deep breath, trying not to overact.

'*He didn't tell me*' she said, her voice sounding a little depleted. Jed took over and asked Frosty to repeat what he had said; what he knew about the guy.

'*So, he never told you?*' he repeated. Sam broke her silence and mumbled a quiet, confused, '*no*'. Jed adjusted himself in his seat, feeling a desperate need to take control of the conversation once again.

'*Ok, tell us what you told him*' He said firmly and Frosty took a final gulp of tea and started to cough before clearing his throat and holding up the empty mug for a refill.

'*Well, I told him that I had heard about a deal coming up, but that was months ago*' Frosty pushed back greasy strands of hair and his fingers slid down his unshaven face as he tried to recall the information he had passed on.

'*erm, yeah, they offered me a chance to make a few hundred quid, if I did a drop ... yeah, it was the drugs first, then ...*'

Jed leaned forward across the table and only moved back slightly when Frosty's mug was refilled and the waitress had walked away.

'*What?*' he barked. Frosty took another mouthful of hot tea and leaned forward himself, so as to keep his voice down.

'*They needed someone to do a drop, few hundred quid and when I spoke to your governor, he asked me to do it and report back, which I did?*'

Sam clasped her hands over her mouth and closed her eyes, Jed quickly glanced at her before pressuring Frosty to continue.

'Yeah, so ...' he began *'I had to meet white van man and he would take me somewhere where I would hand over an envelope; didn't know what would happen after that. In fact, I was told that may be all, but I would be told when I got there?'*

Frosty held out his hands to show he didn't know after that but Jed laid his hand on the table and splayed out his large fingers, speaking firmly but quietly as he watched Frosty retreat.

Jed tapped the table and drew Frosty back to his glare, whispering to him that it was imperative he thought hard about what happened and not to miss anything out.

Sam took her hands away from her mouth, she felt sick at the thought of them being close, *months ago*? Her mind was racing and she desperately wanted to call Jamie and ask him to explain, ask him why he kept this from her? What was she missing, what was he worried about or did he just omit to mention because he had other things that took a priority over finding Grace?

Jed was still questioning Frosty when the café door opened and Frosty silenced and tried to slide lower into his seat to avoid being noticed. Jed looked around and saw an unkempt fellow order a coffee, search for change, then study the room. He felt sure he had noticed Frosty and that split-second moment when he knew better than approach or even acknowledge, he turned and left.

'*Man*' he pleaded '*I'm no good to anyone if I'm made!*' Jed made out they had not been seen, but knew it was not the case.

Sam began to talk fast, everything at once and Jed knew her well to see she was unravelling. He tried to raise his hand, to let her know it was ok, they were just talking and would deal with Jamie later but Sam was jabbering and making little sense.

'*Sam ... stop*' he demanded, causing her to blink hard, then looking into Jed's eyes, she took a deep breath as he whispered '*Two minutes Sam*'

'*You didn't find the kiddie then?*' asked Frosty and at that point the two of them turned to face him.

'*Grace?*' cried Sam. Jed reached out and grabbed Frosty's wrist which at first felt threatening but Jed quietly whispered it was fine, to answer the question and then they could all be on their way.

Frosty looked around the room once more, realising less people were in the café now and asked if they could go elsewhere but Jed refused.

'*No, we are not leaving here until we know what happened, where you went, what you told the Governor, but first did you see Grace?*'

Frosty clenched his fist and tried to retract it but Jed kept a tight hold on it. *'Continue'* he threatened.

'I, err … I went to the station and waited and when he pulled up …'

'*Who?*' snapped Jed.

'I didn't know his name but he had a beard, drove a white van' Frosty answered, then looked at Sam who was trying with every part of her body to keep it together.

'Sir Geoffrey's brother?' she heard herself repeat. Jed was still holding Frosty's wrist but with his left hand he raised his fingers off the table to gesture for Sam to hold back.

'You know him?' Frosty spoke up, but Jed nodded and told him to continue. *'He had me drive with him around London and we picked up another guy who then took over the driving and the toff got in the back'* Frosty cleared his throat again.

'I didn't know what was going to happen to me, honestly, thought it was my lot. One next to me, one behind me; you hear things don't you, see things on tv where they get you from behind. Won't deny I thought I was a gonna, really shit me up!'

Jed swirled his hand in the air until Frosty realised he was digressing. *'Anyway, neither spoke. It was frightening and I asked if I could get out but they didn't talk until I got to the back of Green Street'.*

'Frosty, did you hear about Grace?' Sam

145

couldn't hold back any longer and Frosty started to nod frantically.

'*Yes, maybe ... a kid definitely*' he said and his face was now creasing as he looked terrified of telling them something, they weren't ready to hear.

'*And?*' Sam pushed herself forward across the table as Jed held his arm across, telling Frosty to answer her '*Did you see a child?*' he barked.

Frosty nodded again, closed his eyes momentarily, then when he opened them, he looked a little taken aback, caught by his own emotion.

'*.. alright*' he mumbled. '*no kid should be taken away from their family*' he said and he slumped down, his head on his chest, defeated.

'*Then let us help them?*' Jed added. '*you're not to blame here. You can make a difference and we can make something good come out of this, if you help us?*'

Frost looked up, a tear sat on his lower lid, his eyes darting between their desperate faces.

'*yeah, ok*' he continued. '*I was asked to wait, thought my life was over ...*' Jed butted in. '*yeah, we get that, what did you see or hear when inside?*'

'*An old boy came over, not Sir Geoffrey, he wouldn't be seen talking to the likes of me*' said Frosty. '*He asked if I had something for him and I handed him the package, drugs I thought but he slipped a knife into the package and it was cash ... so much cash*' Frosty's eyes widened.

'He then said; we have a deal then ... great and walked away'. Frosty swiped his cuff across his nose and caught the tear that fell off his cheek.

'I called out to him, stood up you know, got shit scared in the van and called out to him that I had done what I had been asked to do, so could I please go but he waited until he got to the end of the corridor and I thought that was it, but just at that last moment he turned and looked back' Frosty pushed back another wayward greasy strand of hair and drew a breath, before continuing. 'You see stuff where suddenly someone gestures that they have no use for you anymore and I thought that was the moment but ... he looked back and as he spoke; he turned the door handle and it opened. He said they should drop me off, make sure I got far enough away.'

Frosty then turned to Sam, she noticed him swallow hard and he started to blink faster, a nervous twitch took over his lip.

'I could see a little girl in the room' he said but this time his voice was so quiet, nothing else could be heard, the sound of a little girl in a room such as that, had resonance and finality to it.

Sam sat numb, unable to speak. Jed touched her hand but got no reaction whatsoever.

He returned his attention to Frosty and asked him to be specific, as much as possible, and describe her age, colour of hair, anything?

Frosty couldn't take his eyes off Sam but slowly repeated she was young, he thought around 3 or 4, he remembered a white dress but it was at a distance. He noticed she was looking down the corridor at him as the door closed. He also added she wasn't upset, hoping that helped and finally he said he heard Sir Geoffrey's brother in the room speak softly to her as they left.

Jed pushed Sam for the photo of Grace which she managed to pass to him but unfortunately Frosty was unable to be sure, so asked again if he could go.

'Yeah, maybe it's best' said Jed. *'But Frost, we will need to talk again and you will have to go over this a few times I have no doubt, so start writing it down ok'* Frosty nodded in agreement, just desperate to get away. *'Think hard and write it down!'* Jed repeated.

Jed clasped Sam's hand and passed her a tissue with the other. He leaned into her shoulder and whispered to her that all was not lost; in fact, there had been a break through and now they needed to question Jamie.

Sam looked up at Jed as he helped her out from the behind the table.

'We've lost precious months Jed, whatever the excuse, it's not acceptable' Jed agreed but rather than talk further in the café, he escorted her outside, catching the swinging door that Frosty left upon exit.

Daylight caught their eyes as they walked away and headed for Jed's car but it was the sound of vehicles crashing and people screaming that stopped them in their tracks.

'*Stay here*' demanded Jed and passing Sam his keys he ran back down the street. There in the middle of the road lay Frosty. He was motionless and already bystanders were making calls to the emergency services and others were trying to assist a second driver who had been caught in the collision.

Jed knelt down by Frosty's side but realised it was too late. He was laying in a pool of blood; his head injury left him with no chance of survival. His body was twisted like the wreckage that hit him but then Jed looked up at the witnesses; some in distress, mostly shock.

'*Where is the other vehicle*?' he asked. A lady looked in the other direction and pointed but Jed was only able to see a van in the distance and sadly by the time he got his phone out to take a picture it was too far away.

'*Can everyone just stay where you are please*' advised Jed as he tried to help one passer by sit to the side, she felt faint and needed some water.

'*Even if you didn't see the actual accident, please step over here to the pavement. The services are on the way but you may be surprised by what you did notice, so don't leave. Thanks*'.

Sam was walking back towards the scene so Jed stepped away to meet her. His body fully against hers, he asked her to remain calm and then whispered in her ear that it was Frosty.

Police and Ambulance arrived and took control of the situation. Jed left his details with an ex-colleague and said he had been talking with Frosty moments before the accident and would help with their investigation but for now he had to follow a lead and they agreed to let him go.

By the time Jed and Sam reached the Agency, it was hard to contemplate how they were able to move on from this; both in shock and trying not to forget what Frosty had told them, they headed up the stairs together.

Members of their teams greeted them and a couple of close colleagues got up to hug Sam when she passed by, but she didn't loiter. A Saturday called for skeleton staff, but the dedication of the department, left for no closure.

At a distance Jed noted Jamie in his office, his door was closed but he had already seen them approaching.

He wondered what Jamie would make of the information they had been given that morning, or the suspicious timing of Frosty's demise and most importantly what he would have to say for withholding information? Jed's expression gave Jamie prior warning and as he tapped on the boss's door and opened it, Jamie waited a second for Sam to catch up before announcing to them both: '*We need to talk*' then inviting them to sit first.

'*You mean you do!*' snarled Jed.

'*Before you start Jed ...* 'Jamie ordered. '*Sam, I am so sorry that this has come between us. Without comparing, you will never know the difficulty I've had with this*' Jamie stood up, a huge bulk of a man, now asking for her understanding.

Sam was a little emotional and took a tissue from her bag. Jamie slowly lowered himself into his seat, his gaze never leaving hers, but she didn't respond. '*okay, well, let me explain*' he said.

'*Frost's dead!*' exclaimed Jed and with that Jamie silenced, his eyes opened wide and then he gasped aloud. '*When? How?*'

Jed told him about their meeting and that he felt they had been made when another guy left the café but he hadn't expected Frost to be in any immediate danger.

'*Really?*' quipped Jamie. '*You didn't think an informer would look suspicious have tea with you?*' he then whacked the table in front of him, the sound reverberating around the room. '*Jed, we needed him! ... for fucks sake, it's blown!*'

Jed sat forward on his seat; his demeanour clear. '*Still waiting for an explanation*' he replied curtly, his voice louder in frustration but this only led for

Jamie to shout back.

'*Watch your tone Jed!*' and with that the room outside began to stir and concerned faces looked over.

'*Sit down and listen*' he ordered. '*Sam, I told you awhile back that you could have Jed to help you but I also had my reasons and I mentioned I had something going on?*' Jamie implored Sam to back him up and though she looked a little confused momentarily, she acknowledged with a heavy sigh.

'*You knew?*' she questioned. '*You knew Grace could be there? Standing in my home that day, you knew where she was?*'

Jed asked her to give him a moment and then turned his attention once more to Jamie. '*Go on*' he ordered.

'*Frost was working for us at the time, in fact assisting the Police and in particular for child services and they had already got the support of the Court and ... '*. Jed interrupted once more '*... and what?*'

Jamie stood, overshadowing the table.

'*It's not just Grace*' he barked, more from a position of defence than understanding. '*You know how many people go missing every year ... the pair of you do! They asked for Frost to infiltrate. Their concern however was he was known in the area, how much could they risk; but they had no choice.*' Jamie turned and walked over to the window, hands in pockets and with a defeated sigh his chest rose and fell before he turned back to the room.

'When Frost said he had a way in I had already found out that you had been in contact with him and he told me you had left a voicemail Sam? Said he couldn't put you off any longer so I paid you a visit and offered Jed, instead'

Both Jed and Sam listened intently before Jed interrupted once more *'So, you sent me in to do what?'* he asked. *'Start going over stuff and hopefully give Frost time to do his part?'* Jamie nodded.

'Yes, I was told to back off where Frost was concerned, in no uncertain terms. The Police are investigating a few cases and needed him on the inside. I hadn't banked on you getting so far, so quickly, it's only been a few days?' Sam looked at Jed, then back at Jamie; it was true.

Jamie sat down and sipped his water, then looked at Jed, his expression changed.

'I told him to let me know, made it very clear, to let me know if a meet was arranged. I would have intervened; it wasn't enough time and now ... FUCK!!! Now, we have no way back in. Don't you see?' Jamie waved his arms out front at the two of them. *'No Frost, no way in! Police were very clear about that! You think I lost you valuable time before? Now it's gone for good and when the Police find out my team were talking with one of their informers, after they warned me off .... fuck!'*

Sam sat up straight, picked her bag up off the floor and leant on it as she leaned forward and whispered *'Delaying? If I find out Grace had been there …* '. Jed reached over and pressed on her forearm just in time. *'Let's go'*

Jamie walked around the side of his desk and put his arm out to stop them walking past.

'Hold on' he said. *'I need to make some calls'* Jed stepped in front of Sam, his body shielding her from the boss and though he towered over Jed, it was Jamie who withdrew.

'Wait' Sam paused. *'When you came round you said there would be something, I would have to help you with? Was it this?'* Sam looked around Jed's shoulder and as he moved slightly to the side for her to be seen and Jamie stepped back and placed his hands in his pockets once more.

'Partly' he breathed. *'I knew I had been ordered to 'step aside' and that this bust was bigger than just one child … but I knew that this one child was your child, Grace was our priority and I believe that Sam'* and for a moment Jamie looked every bit as vulnerable and helpless as she did.

Jamie continued with his confession. *'I told them I could not … would not, do that but trust me when I say that the powers from above made it very clear that I would be removed altogether so I tried to think of a way of doing both.'* Jamie lowered his eyes to the floor, his body sluggish against the wall.

'*You know, when this interfered with your search, I offered you Jed. That, by the way, has not yet come back to bite me … till now*' he stood straight and removed his hands, before stepping back to open the door.

'*I am on your side Sam, I would do whatever you ask, where I can and yes, I did say there may be something I would ask of you later but honestly, I didn't know what that would be … and here we are?*'

Sam placed her hand on the door and though the office on the other side had become remarkably quiet, she slowly closed it and stepped back.

'*Okay, I get it*' she sighed. Jed looked down at Sam, his frown said it all.

'*Seriously?*' he questioned.

'*Jed*' Sam turned to face him and placing her hands on his chest she pressed just a little.

'*He gave me you*' she replied. '*Look how far we have come in just a few days?*' she pushed him. '*Sit, please, let's sit down and see what we can do from here*'

Jamie gratefully returned to his chair and pulled it out once more and within seconds all three had resumed their positions.

'*I cannot tell you the difference it made having Jed, so thank you*' Sam confirmed, her voice lighter and more hopeful than Jed had heard in a while. She looked sideways to Jed who knew what she was saying was true.

'*We have come so far, honestly, at my darkest time, when I thought I couldn't get any further, you let me have Jed and in the last few days, I cannot believe the route we have taken and I am truly sorry about Frosty, there was something so real there and I now know it has to be explored further*' Jamie attempted to interrupt but Sam put her hand out front.

'*I don't know how, not about to charge in ok*' she assured him. '*Just know that my time with Jed has been clearer than the 6 months previous on my own and it led us to Frosty and the possibility of Grace, well ... someone's little girl anyway ... waiting to be found and that has to be explored? Right?*'

Jamie now clasped his hands in front and rocked back and forth in his seat. He nodded and sighed at the same time.

'*I am so glad Jed made the difference; you will never know how that eases my conscience Sam. It may surprise you to know I have one ... but I do*' A brief smile was shared between the two.

'*Yeah, I am grateful you released me to concentrate on Grace and you know how we battled over that*' he looked to Jamie who was quick to agree. '*But now?*' he sat up straight. '*How do we get in there now?*'

Jamie drew another heavy breath, shrugged his

shoulders and shook his head in despair.

'I wish I knew' he murmured. 'I wish I had the answer, Frost was your way in'

Their silence was broken suddenly with a call from Mia. Sam stared back at the screen, her daughter's name flashing but with the same speed she pulled her phone from her bag, she dropped it back, saying she would call her later.

'Sam, seriously' Jed paused, waiting for Sam to look his way 'You put her off the other day, go speak to her?'

She knew he was right but at this point what would she say? How could she even begin to mention recent events? The last time they spoke, she had arrived at Mia's house to find out Joe had moved out and they had separated. What would she say now when Mia asks if they caught up?

'Go, she must be going through hell and you will just have to choose what bits to miss out ... for now anyway'

Sam rose and looking back at Jamie and Jed before she opened the door, Jed agreed to catch up with her later in the day.

'Okay' Sam relented 'Jed, you must go home too. It's a Saturday for Pete's sake, you have a family who haven't seen you for days!' Sam cocked her head to the side and waited for him to agree.

'Fair enough' Jed smiled in return. 'I will' he

flashed her a smile. *'Go ... I promise I will head home when I am done here'*

Sam was met at the door by Mia who rushed out to the car and grabbed hold of her.

'Oh, thank God' she gasped. *'Why haven't you answered my calls? My texts?'* she cried. *'Darling, I am so sorry'* soothed Sam, trying not to lose control of her emotions so early on. *'Let's go inside'*

Sam pulled Mia's arm and tucked it under hers as they headed back to the house and closed the large front door behind them.

The next hour was lost with emotion, both trying not to accuse the other of being secretive or the fear of not sharing overshadowing the importance of their meeting. Mia kept agreeing as she tried desperately not to interrupt her Mum, pouring out her emotions and trying to offer a positive spin, like *'I have Jed on board now, it's proved so helpful.* And Mia's tears gently falling down her face, grasping small snippets of hope.

She knew Jed was a major force in her Mother's life and had argued early on with Sam that she was not pushing hard enough for Jed full time, even though she could never really appreciate the restrictions they were under.

'Did you catch up with Joe?' Mia asked, her expression one of concern now as she mentioned that she had tried to call him numerous times and

been unable to reach him. Sam paused and looked out the window in a bid to not focus on Mia when she said she had and he was struggling in his own way, however, he had been helpful with their new line of enquiry and Joe and Jed had managed to re-direct the search. She also asked her daughter to please not pressure Joe at this stage and to let them work together, with a promise to get back to her when they were in a better place.

'We will talk soon, I promise' Sam heard herself repeat once more.

Mia knew there was more to know, perhaps she was a little worried to ask, but Sam managed to get their conversation to a stage where Mia accepted Sam was doing her very best. She was able to support that when she explained she had just left a meeting with the Chief of the Agency and Jed was still there. It gave a false sense of security, but security all the same.

Meanwhile Jamie and Jed were trying to find a way back to the club. Jamie had no reason to keep his thoughts to himself and the two spoke openly.

'There must be another contact?' stated Jed.

'Who?' asked Jamie. *'Who now, at short notice, that could possibly get into the club without suspicion? Come on Jed, there will always be a contact out there, sure, but who without looking bloody obvious?'* Jamie held out his hands in question *'I know, we are desperate here; I get it, but with Frost out of action,*

it's the delay?' Jamie sat back in his chair with a slump.

Jed gasped *'Wait'* he said and sat bolt upright.

'What?' asked Jamie *'Tell me?'* Jed stood up *'I have to go'* but Jamie met him at the door.

'Hold on Jed' he said placing his arm across his chest. *'Seriously, you better share whatever it is this time. I cannot help you, or protect you, if you go off half cocked and put yourself or the Agency at risk again?'*

Jed lowered his eyes to Jamie's armed barrier and finally Jamie withdrew. *'You have been warned'* he threatened.

'Loud and clear' he said and left the office with the door swinging behind him.

Whilst he headed down the stairs and out of the building to his car nearby, he felt elated. He knew he couldn't disclose to Jamie Joe's name without highlighting his involvement, not yet anyway. He also knew that he couldn't disturb Sam whilst she was with Mia as Mia didn't know of Joe's involvement.

Jed drove to Joe's apartment at speed and with a little reluctance Joe was forced into the car and the two headed off. He realised Joe was the only other person that had met with the bearded man, the ghost in the picture. A van that Frosty had said pulled up and took him to the club, one driving and one in the back.

Joe met this chap with the drug drop and wouldn't look out of place to any of them; Jed's only concern was that Rick could get to hear that he had been there without his instruction and that could raise suspicion, but for now he had no choice.

Sam was able to leave Mia a little calmer than before, with the promise of keeping her updated as soon as she could and Mia realised there was a lot more her mother needed to do, leaving her with no choice but to trust her implicitly.

Sam tried calling Jed but he was not answering his phone and after leaving a voicemail Sam decided not to attempt again. After all, she had insisted he went home and spend time with his family so it felt unfair to disturb him. A voicemail would have to do she thought and turning the key to her apartment, Sam drew a deep sigh and leant against the inside of the door.

She was exhausted and knew this nightmare was going to beat her in the end; but please God let it be worth it; accepting nothing less than the safe return of Grace.

Day 5 – Sunday (early hours)

It was dark and in the very early hours of Sunday morning Sam was woken by a telephone call. She was startled initially and a little unaware of her surroundings. Waking up on the sofa should be something she was used to by now, but it threw her.

It was a call from the Hospital and Sam tried desperately to focus. It was Mia and they were advising her she was stable and that she had been brought into Hospital earlier that night and now sleeping it off.

'*Sleeping it off?*' Sam repeated, her voice quickening. '*What was it? An overdose?*' The Nurse asked Sam to listen, she stressed Mia was fine, they believe she had taken more sleeping tablets than necessary but certainly not enough to be an overdose.

'*Has she been under any pressure lately*?' the Nurse asked. Sam nearly laughed, she held back her need to release.

'*Yes, immense pressure*' she confirmed, then said she would make her way to the Hospital immediately, asking they let Mia know.

'*No rush*' the Nurse continued '*Like I said she will need to sleep this off, so no rush*'

The streets were pleasantly quiet as Sam made her way to the Hospital. Her little car chugged along, but it got less use lately as she was mostly home and when out and about, Jed drove.

She made her way through the silent corridors and was by Mia's side, relieved to be holding her hand, collapsing over her daughter's tiny frame.

Mia was in a side room thankfully and when the Nurse popped by to see her, she was able to re-assure Sam once more that it was their opinion Mia had taken a little more than she needed, causing her to fall into a deeper sleep. She was also able to confirm that Mia called the Ambulance herself, stating her concern and that she couldn't remember how many she had taken but was struggling to stay awake; something the Nurse said was a good indication of her state of mind and not a cry for help.

Sam laid her head against Mia's hand and before long drifted off to sleep, aware that her daughter had been furthest from her thoughts in recent months.

Around 5am the Nurse appeared in the doorway and asked Sam if she would like a cup of tea, which she gratefully accepted.

Mia was checked and her vitals were good, she had stirred a little and although very groggy she was able to recognise her Mum and squeezed her hand when prompted.

Sam's phone broke the silence in the room and searching through her bag frantically so as to not disturb Mia, she quickly rose and walked to the large window and whispered hello. She hadn't noticed Lisa's name on the screen in her hurry to answer and when she heard Jed's wife speak, she pulled the phone away from her face and studied the screen for clarity, before speaking her name.

'*Lisa, you ok?*' she said whispered. '*I'm at the hospital and trying to keep my voice down*'

'*Oh, thank God*' Lisa cried '*I hadn't realised you knew and I didn't want to call you too early but it's good you're there*'

'*How did you know?*' asked Sam, a little confused. '*I didn't want to disturb Jed.*'

'*Sam*' Lisa paused for a moment, realising they were talking at cross purposes '*It's Jed, he's in Hospital ... a knife wound?*'

Sam left the room immediately and outside the door she gasped aloud '*What?*' looking back through the window to see Mia asleep.

'*Where is he?*' she pleaded but the phone line broke and crackled so Sam said not to worry, she would find him. Lisa mentioned a particular ward and with that Sam headed off to the Nurses station, asking them to let her daughter know when she woke that she would be back soon and not to allow her to go anywhere without her.

Heading down the corridor Sam's mind was racing. She had last seen Jed at the Agency with Jamie, then he was heading home?

Now she was trying to be quiet, but rushing down corridors and up a staircase, her breathing heavy and her mind racing, '*oh please God no, not Jed*' she begged. Aware he was a young man with a wife and sons, she prayed he would be alright.

Leaving one staircase and turning a corner Sam hurried down the next to be met by Jed, covered in blood and leaving a room that was full of medics. '*Jed*' she called but he rushed towards her and held her back, so as not to see.

'*What are you doing here?*' he asked.

'*You ok?*' cried Sam, her hands on his shirt, pulling it aside to see his injuries.

'*No, it's not me*' he said shaking his head. '*It's Joe*'

Sam stood straight, her eyes widened and her mouth opened slightly before she repeated his name.

'*Joe?*' she said and although still holding on to his clothing, Jed took hold of her hands and clasped them tightly.

'*Yeah, Joe*' Jed repeated, his tone now low, riddled with guilt. '*Sorry Sam ... it was a moment, an impulsive moment*' he tried to explain. '*After Frost, we had nothing and then I remembered Joe knew the ghost guy, remember Frost said he had been in the van with one driving and one behind, remember?*' he looked into Sam's face waiting for her to catch up. He eventually shook her slightly and she nodded *'Yes, yes, I remember'* she said.

'Well, I couldn't tell Jamie obviously, he doesn't know of Joe's involvement in this but I thought if anyone is on to us, you know with Frost meeting us before … the accident, well we have little time to get back in there before it blows …' Jed let go of Sam and he pushed his hair back off his face, blood and sweat mixed, now staining his hands.

'Fuck, what have I done?' he said and slumped against the corridor wall.

Sam walked around him and looked through the glass. There were numerous medical staff attending to Joe and he was covered in blood. There was equipment being erected and so many people trying to save his life.

Just as Sam leaned on the glass a Nurse turned towards her and shook her head, said she was sorry and then pulled the blind closed. Sam leant her forehead on the window and whispered quietly *'Mia's in another room'*

Sam led Jed away to a side room where they were alone, a couple of sofas and a few chairs, along with a tv, which presumably was a family waiting room.

He tells Sam that he collected Joe and asked him to call Rick, asking to see a photo of Grace, an up-to-date one and knowing that every time he pushed, he would be told that he would have to do something, which happened.

Rick said he had a drop coming up and that Joe would soon be reunited with Grace if he completed this last drop within 48 hours. At first Joe over-reacted, got emotional and begged to have Grace now, crying and losing it, but Jed managed to get his attention and Rick told him where and when.

Then Joe was to meet the ghost but this time Jed would follow, hoping the ghost would offer another way in, or at least give them an insight to his life, his family ... something.

Sam listened intently as Jed explained how Joe was left on the corner, eventually picked up by the white van and from what he could see, it was just the one driver.

Jed followed the car and noted Joe being dropped off at the station, the van waited until Joe had returned about half hour later and he saw Joe hand a small rucksack over to him. The van then drove off and Joe walked the opposite way as agreed with Jed. Joe would call Rick to confirm, as per usual and Jed would meet him where they had arranged, leaving Jed to follow the van, which he did.

Jed took the streets carefully, making sure he was not seen, or so he thought. He must have been made because at one point the van pulled over and forced Jed to continue past, trying not to look over at the driver, but as he turned round the next bend, he was aware the van was stationery.

Jed kept his engine running and stood around the corner, waiting for direction and it wasn't long before the bearded guy finished his telephone call and turned towards the road. He threw his mobile into the van and without a break, he looked directly at Jed, who froze.

At that very moment, Jed felt a body close behind him and a deep voice told him to turn around, very slowly. Jed followed instruction and turned around, unable to see the person talking but Jed was aware there was something placed against his back.

He stepped closer to his car and was told to get in, but as he did, he noticed his keys were missing from the ignition.

'*Wait*' he said but the voice told him to shut up and said that what happened next was his fault. Jed couldn't see what that was and then noticed another car pull up in front of him and there was Joe, sitting in the back seat, looking around, terrified

Jed called out to him but he hadn't heard him and he didn't believe he saw him either.

The voice walked away from Jed's car, having

ordered him to not get out; then got into the car in front and Jed was forced to watch as it sped away.

Sam placed her head in her hands *'No, no'* she cried aloud. *'We'll never get her back now'*

Jed dropped to his knees and took Sam's hands *'Please don't say that, please Sam. ... there has to be a way?'*

'But Joe?' Sam exclaimed, looking up at Jed, his face still stained with Joe's blood.

'What could Joe do? He's next to useless Jed? He can't protect himself, let alone from these people?'

Jed dropped to the floor, curling his arms around his legs and cradling them for a minute.

There was a tap on the door and Jed rose quickly, helping Sam to her feet. A Doctor stood in front of them both and Sam began to cry *'Oh no'* she sobbed. The Doctor apologised to them both and directed his voice to Jed as he explained Joe's injuries were too severe and he had lost too much blood. There was nothing more they could do.

Jed held Sam tight and found himself apologising over and over; he had taken them to the edge and had no idea now how to bring them back. Joe was their only way in and now they faced telling Mia that he was dead?

'Mia' Sam blubbered. Jed placed his head on Sam's shoulder and wept.

A few moments passed and Jed's emotions turned to anger. *'That's it'* he said. *'We did all this, waited for Joe to do Rick's bidding, avoiding Police for fucks sake, in the hope of getting Grace back, sorting something out for Joe but now ... well, now we go to Rick ourselves. Tell him what we know? Or tell the Police what we know ... tell the fucking world what we know?'*

Sam stopped crying and blew her nose, wiping her eyes, for she too felt a new sense of rage. *'Go to Rick ourselves?'* she repeated.

'Yeah, hang him out to dry ... let them believe he was helping us, put him at risk?'

'Jose' Sam said, with a sinister tone. *'Jose is our way in. Let me have a moment with her!'* Jed didn't question her reasons, he had nothing else to offer.

Sam left the room in a hurry and headed back to Mia's ward, then over to the Nurses station. She tried to keep the conversation to a minimum, explained she had an emergency. The Nurse was happy to help and promised to look out for Mia, letting her know her Mother had been by her side and would be arranging for her to be taken home once the Doctor had given consent.

After that Sam called Katie, Mia's best friend and asked her to come to the Hospital and sit with Mia until that time.

Jed then rushed ahead of Sam and whilst she finished on the phone to Katie, Jed called for the lift and they hurried to his car.

'I will drop you off later ok' he said *'Your car will be fine here'*

Sam had forgotten about her own car until Jed remarked but then agreed, time was of the essence and who knows what Rick had found out in the meantime.

They were the only ones to know Joe had died and there was only a small window of time before that became common knowledge. The thought of Grace being more at risk, now that Joe was off the scene, was terrifying.

From Rick's point of view, it meant that any blame for Grace's abduction could be dumped on Joe; he would be in the clear and if it hadn't been for the fact that Joe had opened up to Sam and Jed, no-one would have thought Joe had turned to a drug dealer for help?

Sam held on as Jed's car lurched forward and turned hard on the next bend, leaving the Hospital car park in the distance.

'Easy' Sam begged him. Jed gave a sideways glance to Sam, then acknowledged her by slowing down.

'We should have asked for his phone' Sam continued and with that Jed struggled to reach inside

his jean pocket and produced an old Nokia phone, a flip phone that Joe refused to update.

'*What?*' Sam exclaimed. '*How the hell?*' but before she could say anything else Jed told her that when Joe called him, the phone was on the road beside him; he was unconscious so he picked it up.

Sam opened up the screen as Jed drove, then looked down and gasped '*… it's Joe's blood*' she said quietly.

Jed looked over, then with a puzzled expression he told Sam to wait and pulled his car over to a halt.

'*What is it?*' Sam asked, with panic in her voice.

'*It's just that … hold on*' he continued. Jed then proceeded to take his own phone from his pocket and call the Hospital. He asked to speak with the Doctor once more and was relieved when the same voice agreed to take his call.

'*Sorry Doc, I am so sorry to disturb you but I need your help please?*' Jed explained. '*It could help with the investigation and the Police will need to know …*'

The Doctor interrupted Jed '*okay, how can I help?*'

Jed described the scene and how Joe was laying on the ground when he approached and the Doctor made agreeable sounds, confirming he understood.

Jed asked specifically about the timing and was

taken aback when the Doctor suggested Jed speak with the person who called it in?

Sam and Jed looked at each other, the phone held out between them.

'It was Joe who called?' Jed replied.

'Impossible' the Doctor responded. *'He was unconscious and had been for at least an hour or more'*

Sam gasped and held her hand over her mouth whilst Jed drew his breath, then thanked the Doctor for his help.

'Is that all?' he asked. *'Yes, for now, thank you so much'* said Jed, ending the call.

'So, he was dumped there?' realised Sam *'Just like that?'*. Jed nodded.

'But don't you see?' he looked to Sam. *'That means the blood-stained finger prints on Joe's phone aren't his?'* Jed pointed at the phone in Sam's hands and with that she dropped it into her lap.

'We have the killer?' she gasped, her eyes wide and now a smile across her face. *'His prints are on it? We have to hand it to the Police Jed ... right now'*

Jed was silent, facing forward and nodding. *'hmmn'* he murmured. *'We will keep it safe, for sure, but just for the moment we have very little time and need to get to Jose before Rick gets wind of Joe, okay?'*

Jed passed Sam a small plastic bag for the phone to

be placed inside, then they agreed to continue to the apartment block.

As they pulled up on the corner Sam grabbed Jed's arm as she noticed Rick leaving the building and walking around the side. She knew this is where he kept his car and within seconds he drove out and roared up the high street.

'*Come on*' said Sam and the two headed through the main doors and hurried up the stairs, Sam ahead of Jed and initially tapping on Jose's door quietly.

It took a few moments but eventually Jose opened the door slightly and asked Sam what she wanted. Jed must have been just out of sight for the first few minutes of Sam trying to encourage Jose to open the door and he became increasingly frustrated; finally showing himself and stopping Jose shutting the door.

'*I'll break it down*' he promised and with that Jose unchained the door.

It was then that Sam saw her swollen stomach. '*How* many months are you?' she enquired as Jed scoured the room.

'*Don't touch anything*' panicked Jose. '*He will know*'. Her body language was one of fear and she was fidgeting terribly, enough so that Sam tried to calm her and assure her they meant her no harm. It was desperation that brought them to her and this time they needed answers; they had run out of options.

Jed turned to Jose and snapped her out of it. *'Where has Rick gone?'* he barked. *'Come on, you hear things, so where has he gone? Who is he meeting? ...'* he waited for a reply but Jose looked between the two of them, her eyes darting back and forth and her bottom lip started quivering?

'He didn't say' she attempted but Jed barked once more and stepped forward in a manner that caused Jose to step back and stumble.

'Jed!' snapped Sam. *'Hold up!'* Jose righted herself once again and started to cry quietly *'Please leave?'* she begged.

Sam reached out for Jose's hand and to her surprise she took it, still watching as Jed rummaged around the room.

'Listen Jose' Sam began slowly. *'I mean you no harm and you have to agree I could have gone to the Police with what I already know; you know how Rick and Joe started this? They could see you as an unfit mother and you could lose your child?'*

Jose whipped her hand away. *'Please, I haven't done anything'* she cried. *'I can't lose another baby; I won't let you'* she sobbed.

Sam perched against a chair, there were items everywhere. The room smelt so bad, remnants of drink and drugs covering most surfaces and in the far corner there was a basket of baby bits. It was the smallest area possible in the crowded room and from the layout it was most precious to Jose.

Sam stared momentarily and felt Jose look over, then back.

'*I lost my last baby*' she repeated. '*A little girl, still born*' she said, her voice frail and in pain. Sam once more leaned towards her and tried to calm her.

'*Rick isn't a good role model Jose. Rick a father? He can't provide for a family like this?*' and with that Jose followed Sam's hand as she surveyed the room.

'*He's desperate for a kid*' Jose insisted. '*It broke him last time, you don't know him like I do?*'

Sam agreed, fair enough, she didn't but she knew this wasn't the way to live and she also reminded Jose that she had witnessed may rows, seen the bruises and injuries and how was she going to protect a child?

Jose continued to defend Rick, saying that when her baby was born, he had arranged everything; he didn't leave her to deal with it on her own.

'*Which Hospital?*' asked Sam, trying to keep Jose's attention away from the fact that Jed was now opening drawers and cupboards.

'*No Hospital*' Jose told her. '*We had a room set up at Sally's*'

Jed stopped his search *'Sally down the end?'* he bellowed. Sam looked over at Jose and realised how vulnerable she was.

'So, you had the baby in Sally's apartment?' she clarified and Jose nodded, saying they had everything in place and Sally had been really helpful. When they realised, they were losing the baby Sally had given her something for the pain, helped her sleep through the difficult time.

'Did you see the baby?' Sam asked, keeping her voice and tone more as an interested enquiry, as opposed to an accusation.

Jose shook her head *'No, that's what I mean. Rick insisted it should be taken care of and not for me to worry'*

Sam gestured to Jed to continue his search and then turned her attention once more to Jose.

'Darling, I'm not sure I believe the baby died' she said, but unfortunately Jose cried more and begged them to leave.

'Not yet' Sam apologised. *'Listen to what I have to say for a minute ok'* and whilst Jose wept quietly Sam described the situation and her belief that perhaps (just perhaps) Sally had enabled Rick to make a deal for her baby.

Jose continued to deny the idea and occasionally she pointed to the door and cried louder, continuously begging them to leave.

Jed made his way over to the women and shouted. '*Enough!*' Both Jose and Sam looked up.

'*Right, Jose, you tell us now … every fucking thing you know and if not, I am going to tell Rick that you gave him up, that you told us he and Joe were working together and whether you were directly involved or not, the Police will not let you keep this baby when they know you enabled an abduction*'

'*NO!* yelled Jose. '*I didn't have anything to do with Grace being taken!*' she squealed.

'*But you didn't do the right thing either, did you?!*' shouted Jed. '*You let someone take Sam's little girl, that didn't bother you? It's different now it's yours eh?*'

Jose lowered herself to the floor and sat in a huddle. '*No, I never hurt Grace. I begged Rick not to do it, I promise, I promise you from the bottom of my heart*'

Sam found herself unable to look at Jose, the emotions of a young naive girl begging for forgiveness, yet the only link to finding out what happened to her granddaughter. Jed called Sam's name and raised his voice again.

'*Tell her!*' he snapped. '*Rick could be on his way back Sam. It's now or never.*' He continued. '*You said you would do a deal with devil?*' he shouted and Sam looked startled by his tone.

'*Well?*' Jed bellowed. '*The Devil comes in all guises*' and with that he pointed at Jose's pathetic frame in the corner.

Sam bent down and leaning forward, she whispered to Jose that this was the end. She told Jed to get ready to call Rick and Jose began to cry once more.

'I will do all I can to get your child taken away from you Jose, everything ... you will know what it is like to lose your child, have them taken away by some low life and feel helpless, unless you help us now; this very minute!'

Jose looked at Sam, her eyes full of tears, then up to Jed who had rage staring back.

'He got a call' Jose began *'Said he would be there in 20 minutes and I don't know who he was talking to ok ...'* her voice trailed off but Sam encouraged her to continue, stroking her arm as she helped her to feet.

'He was talking about you I think' she pointed to Jed. *'Said he would deal with wonder boy himself! He was swearing and when he ended the call, he said he should never have let Joe in ... called him a fake '*

Sam praised her for helping and asked her to think about other calls, other contacts, any other visitors but Jose started to frown, her mind full of questions now.

'Do you really think my baby was given away?' she looked to Sam, praying she would take back the suggestion?

Sam could have continued berating her but found herself feeling for her; her trust in Rick now in question.

'*I wasn't there*' she said, in the hope of keeping communication open between them. '*You could speak with Sally?*' she suggested. '*She would be able to tell you exactly what happened?*' but before she could complete the rest of that sentence Jed shouted across the room that Sally was not to be trusted.

'*She would do anything for money!*' he protested, then realised Sam was still working hard to instil trust between them.

Jose nodded, saying nothing, just nodding and staring blankly ahead.

'*Do you have any idea about Grace or where she is now?*' Sam whispered. '*Do you know if she is alive? Please … help me?*'

'*I'm having a boy*' Jose muttered and at first Sam looked confused but straight after Jose recalled the moment she went into labour.

'*We knew it was a girl*' she said. '*Sally kept saying girls are trouble and Rick had said a few times that he wanted a boy … do you think he gave my baby away because it was a girl?*'

Sam tapped her hands. '*Jose, concentrate, please?*' she implored. '*What do you know about Gracie? Anything?*'

Jose broke her stare and looked into Sam's eyes. '*She is alive*' she said. With that Sam took a gasp and stumbled back; words she had only dared to hope for, but time gave way to doubt. '*Are you sure?*' she cried. '*Jose, can you be sure?*'

Jose showed a small smile for the first time and the warmth she felt from Sam's obvious relief was comforting.

'*I have been keeping track*' she whispered. '*I found something*' she said and pointed to a painting at the far end of the apartment. '*Yes, behind there*' she confirmed.

Jed pulled forward the picture and, in the wall, a small area of concrete had been removed and a book sat; he glanced back at Sam as he gently removed it.

Sam squeezed Jose's hand and thanked her. '*Bless you*' she whispered. '*Do you know where Grace is now?*' she repeated, her cheeks wet from tears and her voice breaking, with a little emotion and relief, trying to keep control she asked the question again.

'*Not for sure*' Jose answered. '*The book has addresses*' she confirmed. '*I've only looked a couple of times as Rick would know and he only gets it out when he thinks I'm asleep*'

Jed held it against his chest after looking through the first few pages.

'It's everything' he told Sam. 'Let's go'

Sam looks about the apartment, so much has been disturbed by Jed 'We can't leave it like this' she said, her hand sweeping out before her

'Look!' Jose pulls her arm 'It's ok' she tells her. 'I will say I had a meltdown, but please, you must go' she begs.

Jed made his way past the sofa and pushes paperwork back onto the seat, believing it to have been there when they arrived. Sam raised her eyes; aware Jose is in real danger but Jed quickly reminded her 'No more than we are if Rick finds us here!'

Jed went ahead of Sam and checked to see if Sally was about, then Sam opened the door of her own apartment and the two disappear inside.

Sam takes the book from Jed and starts flicking through, reading names aloud, the two of them trying to decipher abbreviations in the margin.

Suddenly a call comes through and Jed walks away from Sam to answer. She could hear Jamie on the phone and he was pretty vocal; insisting the two of them come to the office as soon as possible; the Police were present and wishing to speak with Jed in regard to Joe.

He says he has vouched for Jed for the time being and given the Agency as a reason for Jed's involvement, confirming Jed would make his way to the

Station tomorrow.

Jed finished the call and looked over at Sam; she knew what she had been asking of Jed these past few days

'It's serious' she pointed out but Jed knew that 'We can't lose momentum now' he explained and Sam sighed with relief, grateful he was so invested.

'Listen' she handed the book to Jed. 'It can't stay here; Jose may give me up' she said. 'Take it home with you, make some sense of it?' Jed paused, then tapped the book in his right hand. 'It's been a day eh?'

Sam smiled 'Could not have done it without you' she smiled and leant in for a hug.

'I've had a text to say Mia is fine and home, Katie will stay with her tonight and I will see her tomorrow' Sam continued as she pulled away.

'Some good news, finally' he said and returning a smile, he headed for the door.

'You can't stay here alone?' he insisted. 'You have to come! Stay at ours, we need to go through this tonight?' but Sam shook her head.

'I know how close we are and the time is now, but seriously, if it kicks off next door, I need to be here to call the Police ... I can't leave her on her own, not now?'

Jed shook his head in dismay *'She deserves what she gets for her part in this Sam'*

Sam reflected on that later but it was enough that they had a major piece of evidence in their possession. She just could not walk away, leaving Jose to fend for herself tonight. They put her in danger and whatever the rights and wrongs of the situation, she couldn't help feel that Jose could still play a pivotal part in the bringing down of Rick and his associates. What she knew could make all the difference.

Before bed Sam spoke to Mia and it was a comfort to hear her apologise for her error, telling her Mother that it was the furthest thing from her thoughts. She couldn't leave Grace, not whilst there was even the slightest hope she would return.

Sam so wanted to give her hope tonight but false hope would be unforgiveable thing at this stage. She told her daughter that she felt closer than ever and asked her not to lose faith.

'Never' Mia whispered. *'We will talk soon and I will explain'* Sam assured her *'I promise. I know I keep saying that, but soon okay?'*

Tonight, was the not the time to mention Joe ... but as his next of kin Mia would be contacted in the morning. Due to her daughter's fragile state, Mia had bought herself a few precious hours when the hospital agreed for Sam to talk with her after she had rested.

Day 6 - Monday

Sam was woken in the early hours and it was clear Rick was in a rage. There were squeals from Jose, furniture being shunted about, or possibly thrown. Shouting between the two had woken up the apartment block by now and at one-point Sam was sure she heard Sally scuttle past and soon after heard her distinctive voice.

'*You took my baby*!' she heard Jose scream. '*You helped him*!' she cried, then Sally shouted back.

'*Shut your mouth*!' she shouted '*Shut her up*!' she continued and, in that moment, Sam grabbed her mobile, unlocked it and was just about to dial for the Police when she heard Jose begging.

'*Tell me?*' she was sobbing. '*Did my baby die? Did you take my baby?*'

Sally shouted again for her to be quiet and then Rick was heard trying to muffle her cries.

'*Get off me!*' Jose fought back and there were sounds of a slap and loud thuds as things landed on the floor, possibly Jose? Sam covered her own eyes and cried silently '*please no*'

But to her surprise and relief she heard Jose once more rise up shouting. '*I know you took my baby … she didn't die, did she? She didn't die?*'

'*Tell her!*' shouted Rick and Sam stood back

from her door, shocked to hear Rick demanding Sally told her? *'Tell me!'* Jose screamed. *'Where's my baby?'*

Sally's evil voice took strength in Jose's weakness and her old frame still gave volume in the night.

'She went to a better home!' she shouted. *'You weren't fit enough to be a mother!'* she exclaimed.

Jose was then heard wailing *'Noooo'* she was crying aloud. *'You let her take our baby!'* then there was the sound of fighting as Jose must have been lashing out.

'Stop!' he demanded. *'We have a boy coming!'* he tried to convince her to stop.

'Are you crazy?' Jose cried as she fought him. *'You gave our girl away you bastard, you gave our girl away and you think you're having anything to do with this baby?'*

Rick could be heard thumping the wall and losing his temper with both of them and finally Sally shouted *'Stop, stop Son, stop right now!'*

Sam leant back against the door *'Son?'* and just as she tried to take that in, she heard Jose exclaim the same *'Son?'* then there was a second of silence before Rick confirmed it was true.

'Girls are a waste of time' Sally shouted. *'My Mother never wanted me, said I should have been given away at birth and I grew up to see that for myself. I wanted the same for my Son; that's all'* she said

in a matter of fact way.

'You fucking witch!' shouted Jose and the sound of Rick trying to grapple with Jose could be heard as she attacked Sally, before Sally was heard slapping her back.

'Hold her arms!' she ordered but Jose must have kicked her as Sally then threatened

'Kick me again and I'll take that kid too!'.

Suddenly Rick changed sides and shouted at his Mother to back off; something he would later regret, she told him.

'That's my Son!' he reminded her. *'go Ma, go now!'*

The door opened and slumped over and shuffling her feet Sam could just make out Sally going past her door, complaining to herself that Rick was a waste of space and no better than his father.

Sam still had hold of the phone, grateful she had not called the Police and knowing Sally's involvement and connections to Rick, it all fell into place and she was in no doubt that Grace had been given away; possibly sold.

Every part of her being wanted to open the door, to grab Sally and drag her into her apartment but she remembered how desperate Joe had been and it would take all her strength not to squeeze the life out of Sally herself.

No, this was a family of spite, disgusting individuals with no moral compass; to deal with them would need a devious plan, but Sam knew who they were now and the part they played in destroying their lives; there was no way they were being handed over to anyone!

She listened while Rick tried to keep Jose in the apartment and although their voices were still loud, with shouting and wailing from Jose, she was surprised to hear Rick begging; telling her he had no choice; he was making a future for them and their son.

By 5am things were quieter and Sam sat up on the sofa, pulling a throw over her shoulders where she must have fallen asleep. She was woken by Jed knocking on the door and she pulled him in with such force he nearly fell on top of her.

'*What's wrong?*' he panicked but Sam locked the door behind him quickly.

'*You won't believe it*' she started and for the next half hour Jed listened as Sam explained all she had heard. Occasionally he found himself repeating '*Sally?*' ... '*Son?*' and then a few expletives.

Sam looked at the book in Jed's hand. '*Any joy?*' she asked, her face hoping desperately for a break through and then Jed smiled.

'*There is something here, it could be Grace ... but I don't know for sure?*' he added finally, his hand out offering the *'please don't bank on it'* plea.

Sam clasped her hands over her mouth and closed her eyes, daring him to repeat his statement.

'No guarantees, but I think I have something; let me show you' Sam pulled up a stool around the breakfast bar and wedged in next to Jed.

For a moment she struggled to see what he was trying to explain, but there was no doubt there was a pattern emerging and some of the initials and abbreviations directed them to a couple of addresses and what they believed was a request for a 3 yr. old?

'What about that one?' pointed Sam. If the same process was used with the same address, then it could be possible that there were 2 children at that address, one 3 yrs. old and another around a year old? Jed agreed

'I'm wondering about Jose now, with what she said about the still birth last year?' he said. *'A complete family; two girls. It's possible?'*

'Surely that can't be happening?' she replied.

'Really Sam?' Jed responded.

There was a postcode and an abbreviated address. Jed told her he had already got someone on it and as soon as he had made sense of it, they could hand it over.

'No' Sam said quickly *'No, please. If it's an ad-*

dress we could take a look ourselves?'

'No need to ask twice' replied Jed. *'I'm right behind you'*

A bang next door caused the two to stop and look towards Sam's door. Then the sound of someone stomping past and heading down the stairs; Sam was first to look out the peep hole and see Rick leaving.

She pressed her finger over her lips and gestured they go quietly to check on Jose. At first Jed felt it was the wrong thing to do but Sam was going, with or without him.

As they knocked on Jose's door, Jed kept watch the other end of the corridor for Sally to surface but Sam was hopeful it was too early for her.

Eventually Jose opened the door and the two entered.

'Are you ok?' Sam asked, reaching forward to hold Jose who in return fell into Sam's arms, weeping.

'Does he know about the book yet?' Jed was quick to check but thankfully Jose said he didn't. She was still shocked that Sally was his Mother and Sam told her she had heard much of the fight.

'You were right' Jose whimpered *'They took my baby. They took my little girl away'* she cried. *'So, I do know what it feels like'*

Sam empathised with her and told her they would do whatever they could to help her but now they needed to find Grace.

'*What about Joe?*' asked Jose.

'*Joe?*' came their joint reply.

'*Well, Joe is her father?*' she questioned. '*Rick was saying we could move away, make a new future for ourselves and that it can't be an abduction, as Joe is her father?*'

Jed bit his lip, unable to hear the nonsense coming from her mouth and seeing that Rick had managed to talk her round, fuelled his anger. Sam saw his reaction and moved him aside.

'*Jose*' she started. '*Joe is dead!*' Jose stepped back, then sat down abruptly.

'*Dead?*' she squealed. '*How?*' Sam perched on the armchair and told her that she couldn't discuss that right now; but it was important to know that the organisation Rick has been involved in goes far beyond her little girl being given away.

Not all children will be given to childless couples for cash; in fact, there is every chance that a child will be sold to a paedophile ring, they can be trafficked and lost forever and her baby's father had been instrumental.

Jose looked to the floor, she could see how Rick was implicated and even her, to a point, knowing he was involved in one abduction was enough to incriminate her; saying she didn't know of any others, however true, wasn't something that would help her or her baby.

'I thought it was drugs … just drugs' she professed.

'Even so, now you know and you knew about Grace, that is enough wouldn't you say?' suggested Sam.

Jose held her stomach and rubbed it gently. *'I can't lose another baby'* she whimpered.

'Hey, look at this' Jed called out and as Jose turned her attention there was another knock on the apartment door. The three of them stood silent and eventually Sally called out for Jose to let her in.

'I know you're not alone' she said. *'You better let me in or I will call him right now!'*

Sam shook her head and Jed signed to Jose not to open the door but Sally called out again and instructed her to open the door or she would call Rick. Jose said she was coming and Sam and Jed stood side by side as Sally entered.

'So' Sally said, her smug smile and wheezing voice breaking the silence. *'What have we here?'* she grinned.

There was no reply from any of them as Sally started to break down what she knew, what she had seen and how this was going to end badly for all of them, but especially Jose when Rick found out she has betrayed him.

'*That's no loss*' came Jed's reply. '*Piece of scum like that in her life, he's no loss*'

Sally smirked and with her long cardigan wrapped around her body, she placed her hands inside her pockets and started to cough, not even attempting to cover her mouth as she did.

'*You're in the wrong place to argue*' she told Jed. '*I've watched you come and go and wondered when this slut would betray my son and here we are ...*'

Jose stepped forward but Sam got between her and Sally.

'*No Jose, she's not worth it, believe me. She's looking for a reaction, she just mentioned an argument, don't give her one*'

Sally cackled and pulling out a knife from her pocket, Sam pushed back on Jose to open up the space between them. Jed stepped forward, pulling them both back.

'*Really*?' Jed smirked. '*What are you going to do with that*?' he taunted. '*I could knock you down in one go*' but as soon as he threatened her, Sam ordered him to stop and told Sally to leave immediately, but she refused.

Sam held out her hands while the room waited for someone to move. Jose was caught in a dangerous position and Sam had never meant to endanger her.

Jose backed away from Sam and Jed, who was still ready to attack, but held firm. In his hand he held a couple of tickets and waved them in front of her face.

'Your son was leaving you!' he blurted out and again Sam flashed him a look. Jed ignored her this time and once more took delight in waving the evidence; Jose could only look on confused.

'Yeah' Jed continued to taunt *'You weren't even in his future, so what do you make of that, eh? Twisted old bat!'*

Sally started to cackle with laughter once more, waving the blade out front and pointing in Jose's direction initially, then out towards Jed and Sam.

'You think those were for her?!' she spat. *'Don't be ridiculous … he knew what she was, she was never in **our** future!'* Jose flashed a look to Jed, then to Sam in hope of an answer but Sam stood frozen.

'Who were they for?' came Jose's feeble reply.

'Not you!' Sally laughed. *'We've planned this for a while now, but you got preggers with the wrong brat … then, as it happens, we got a good offer and put some cash away!'*

Jose gasped *'My little girl?'* and Sally laughed a little louder.

'What a waste of space you are' Sally started animating and her arms were waving with the blade catching in the light; Sam moved forward a

little.

Sally snapped *'Stay back!'* she spat. *'This is all your fault; you just couldn't let it go, could ya?'*

Sam held her hands out in front suggesting they calm the situation. *'Please, put the knife down; just for a minute, lower your hand?'* but Sally scoffed once more and waved it towards Jose.

'Stop moving' Sally barked, then turned her glare to Jed. *'and you wonder boy'* she cackled loudly *'wonder boy? I told him you were no wonder boy'* she snorted and quickly cuffed snot from her nose *'wonder boy, my arse!'* she continued. *'You just couldn't keep your nose out eh? Look what happened to Joe? You did that, didn't ya? Sent that pathetic father off to his death? And for what? Hey? Your kid is long gone .... Pathetic lot!'*

Sam felt anger rise in her stomach but before she could react Jed moved and there was a moment where Sam thought she had lost hope of keeping him back.

'Wait' she bellowed and as Jed came past her, she caught his arm and pulled him with such a force, he stumbled to the left, onto the coffee table and had to rise quickly to regain his stance.

'Wait, wait Jed!' Sam ordered. *'Hold up!'* and as Jed stood straight once more Sally laughed so loud, this time the knife only inches away from Jose.

'Go on, wonder boy, let's see if you can get here before I make my next move?' but this time Jed raised his hands and said OK, 'steady'.

'So' resumed Sally. 'What will Rick make of this then, eh?' then looked at Jose. She was lost, fragile, broken and totally devastated.

'Pathetic, isn't she? Mother material? Huh! I don't think so' she quipped.

'And you are?' Jed blurted out, once again Sam caught his arm.

Sam tried again 'Sally, we need to resolve this' she began. 'What can we do to resolve this, tell us?'

Sally frowned, but there was no confusion, just bewilderment that Sam thought this was even possible to resolve?

'You really are a waste of space' she told her. 'Does your daughter feel proud of her husband; the child napper? You look at my family with disgust but hey, your son-in-law did the kidnapping?' she spat. 'And you judge my son!'

Sam wanted desperately to tell Sally just how disgusted she felt about her son-in-law but he had paid the ultimate price for his betrayal.

'We will see what Rick says when he gets here' Sally said, this time her smile was sly. She had already called him when she saw Sam and Jed enter the apartment. Jose looked terrified to hear that and started to whimper; but Sally threatened her through gritted teeth,

'Your tears won't save you this time; shut up!'

Jed heard feet on the stairs and gestured to Sam that Rick was coming so Sam took the opportunity of moving an inch or two towards Jose and could nearly reach her.

Sally was grinning, her brown teeth on show. She looked so pleased with herself and as Rick burst into the room she laughed, her head tilted back, crowing with pleasure. *'Daddy's home!'*

'Ma' Rick shouted as he burst in, then looking at the room and back to Sally he told her to lose the knife.

'That's my kid' he demanded but no sooner than the words had left his mouth, his mother's look put him in his place and his tone changed instantly.

'Ma? What's going on? Why are they here?' he asked, this time calm and collected.

'Good question' Sally replied, looking at Jose and waving the knife as she spoke.

'Do you want to tell him, or shall I?' she snapped.

Rick turned his stare to Jed; his face began to change and his expression one of anger. Sam could see Jed glaring back; the two were locked.

Sally interrupted, telling Rick that Jose had been

helping them and she wasn't to be trusted. Rick didn't take his eyes off Jed the whole time; he made sounds acknowledging Sally's statement, but didn't reply.

Jed slowly held up the tickets in his hand and with his lip slightly raised with a smirk, he waved them in front of Rick.

'*Off on your Holi bobs*?' he grinned. '*With ya old Ma?*' he continued. '*That's not fucked up eh?*' and with that Rick made his move.

It was difficult to say who did what after that, the room exploded as Rick and Jed became embroiled in a full-on fight; flying over and through furniture, the noise was immense and there was screaming from Jose and shouting from Sally.

Sam made her move and stood over Jose but not before Sally lunged. Sam pushed the old lady back with such a force she nearly keeled over completely but managed to find her feet and come back like some demented she devil.

She was crying like a banshee, her arm high in the air, lashing out in front of her.

'*You're going to die with your brat!*' she yelled.

Rick had grabbed hold of Jed now and the two were crashing back towards the other end of the apartment, fists flying and their bodies being beaten, the noise was unbearable.

Sam was shouting for help as Sally came once

more with the knife. She managed to push the chair towards her and it gave her a second to grab the lamp from the table and swipe it in front of Sally's arm, knocking the knife to the floor.

It fell and could not be seen now that furniture was in disarray and initially Sally looked to the floor, but not seeing it immediately, she grabbed a half-full glass of beer and lobbed it; Jose took the impact and the stale contents covered her face and chest.

Jed got the better of Rick and he began to squeal; calling for his Mother to help and she started to climb over furniture and wade through the debris to get to him.

Sam turned to Jose who was trembling and holding her thigh, close to her stomach, Sam realised she had been stabbed. Jose was crying and shaking;

'Is it my stomach?' she wailed. Sam was shaking her head furiously *'No, no it's your leg'* she cried. *'Put pressure on it, wait here'* she insisted and turned to help Jed.

He was on top of Rick now and pummelling hard, his fists coming down on him like a sledgehammer and his bloody hands, covering Rick's face.

Sally was above, thumping Jed in the back of the head but with one swipe he knocked her backward and Sam was close enough to drag her even further; Jose could be heard screaming that she needed an ambulance.

Rick held his hands out and for a moment it felt like Jose's distress was enough to wake him up. Jed stopped, rose up from Rick's body and turned back to Jose who was covered in beer and blood.

Sam pulled Sally to her feet but her legs were still kicking out at Jed; her mouth still spouting obscenities at them.

'She's better off dead' she was yelling. *'We don't need either of them'* she called over to Rick. Rick tried getting up but he was battered and bruised and stumbling. He could see Jose holding her stomach and sobbing and a rage came over him

'Not my kid!' he shouted and before anyone could react or move, he turned to the drawer and pulled out a gun, aimed it at Sam and Sally and pulled the trigger.

The sound was deafening and both fell to the floor. Sam was still holding Sally as they keeled over, the force of the bullet shot them backwards and into the fireplace.

'Sam!' screamed Jed and he scrambled over the upturned furniture to pull Sally off Sam, then relief to find her unharmed. It was Sally who was clutching her stomach and coughing up blood.

'You waste of space' she spat, blood flying out of her mouth as Rick rushed over.

'You made me do it!' he cried, wiping his hair

back from his face, blood and tears smearing his skin. He still had the gun in his hands as he broke down sobbing over his Mother while Jed pulled Sam to her feet and took her closer to Jose who was crying uncontrollably and at the same time trying to keep pressure on her wound.

'*Ma*' Rick wailed '*Hold on*' but even as he bent down to support her Sally's last words were cruel and evil.

'*Should have got rid of you at birth*' she whispered him. Rick sobbed, tried to sit her up but she told him not to touch her.

'*Go raise your bastard*' she spat, her blood splattering his face as she spoke. Rick shook his head in despair.

'*What did I ever do to you?*' he cried. '*Hey? What did I ever do wrong?*' Sally put out her hand and pulled his face towards her and he willingly leaned in, still hoping for something, a little comfort perhaps at this desperate time.

The second gun shot was muffled; Rick slumped on top of his Mother. She had pulled the trigger between them. Even now Rick could not escape her.

Jose squealed and Sam and Jed stopped her moving from the corner; with Sam continuing to press her wound, instructing Jed to call for an ambulance.

The room was in disarray. Two dead bodies slumped in the fireplace and three witnesses.

Jed looked at Sam and then Jose who felt light headed. '*What are we going to do*?' she cried in fear.

Sam stroked her hair from her face and with a soothing voice spoke slowly and calmly.

'*It's going to be ok*' she assured her. '*We will say you found out Rick was involved in the abduction of Grace and told me, ok*?' Jose nodded, hanging on to her every word.

'*Yeah, and when we arrived …* 'Jed continued. '*Sally came, just like she did and Rick followed, just like it happened and the fight, shooting etc, just like it did*' Jed repeated, nodding furiously, hoping Jose was taking it all in. She was agreeing but then her eyes widened

'*What about Joe*?' she asked in a panic.

'*Joe's dead Jose*' Sam interrupted. '*Can we leave him out of this for now please*?' she begged. '*For my daughter's sake and for Grace's sake. She doesn't need to think badly of her father. He was desperate and gave his life trying to get her back*?'

Jose looked over at the fire place, then into Sam's eyes. '*I can say I don't know or …* 'Jed waved the book.

'*You found this*?' he suggested, '*you told Sam you had information that could help and gave Rick up? After that just keep repeating that you don't know anything else? You know Rick was in to drugs, didn't know about anything else and yesterday found* out that Rick and Sally gave your baby away?' Jed was smiling, waiting for Jose to acknowledge and finally she did.

'Yes, that was unforgiveable, a good mother would give him up, wouldn't she?'

Sam gave a comforting smile and once more pushed a strand of hair from Jose's face. 'Absolutely' she soothed.

From a distance there were sirens, then many feet climbing the stairs. Jed headed for the apartment door and within minutes the room was bursting with uniformed figures.

Paramedics helped Jose out of the room and Sam told her she would make her way to the Hospital later on.

'You have things to do' Jose accepted. 'Maybe you will see what you can do for me too?' she asked, her face childlike and innocent, yet free from fear. Sam placed her hand on Jose's arm 'Goes without saying' she said.

Jed was talking with one of the officers 'So, the boss said you would be coming in today?' he smirked, looking around at Jed's latest handy work 'Got a little way laid, did we?'

The Agency had a strong relationship with the Police and along with Jed's time in the force, they were well known, but dead people were stacking up!

Jed finally looked down at his clothes and there were blood stains on his hands too. The officer also noticed and when their eyes met again, he cocked his head to one side *'This can't wait Jed ... seriously, you have to come to the station'*

'No problem' Jed promised. *'Sam and I will go in my car'* Sam looked over to Jed. *'Just remembered, my car is still at the Hospital?'* she added.

'Hospital?' came the Officer's reply.

'Yes, my daughter was admitted but she's fine now'

Jed greeted a few more officers before leaving the scene and turning at the door he handed over the book *'This is what Jose found'* he said. *'It has all sorts in it, so please don't let it out of your sight'*

Once in the corridor Jed grabbed Sam's arm and rushed them down the stairs and out of the building.

'Quick, quick' he chanted as they took the steps in twos. Sam was still trying to get her thoughts together as other Police and crime scene investigators passed them by in the lobby.

Climbing into Jed's car, the pair looked at each other, unable to dissect all the information; but turning the key and roaring off Sam spoke first.

'We needed the address?' she exclaimed.

'I have it' Jed replied. *'It's engraved in my*

mind, trust me, at 2am this morning I worked it out and nearly broke down their door!'

Sam sighed and placing her hand tenderly on the back of Jed's neck, she smiled, a warm tear left her eye and dropped onto her cheek.

'I owe you everything' she managed to whisper.

Jed pulled her hand from his shoulder and kissed it gently, then concentrated on the road he took them further and further away to a leafy suburb on the other side of town.

As they pulled up, Sam commented on the greenery *'It's beautiful'* she whispered.

'In all my darkest moments, terrifying dreams, I have prayed … just prayed that she had been given to a family who wanted to love her, not harm her' Sam couldn't hold back her emotions.

Jed tried to comfort her, asking her to hold on. There was no guarantee this was the place. He had felt confident at 2am this morning, working on the abbreviations and clues in the book, but there were guarantees.

What if she had been here initially? A safe house, as it were … it was out of the way for sure. She could have been listed as delivered here, only to be moved on or worse still, sold?

Sam paused and Jed asked her to wait while he took a closer look.

Moments passed and Jed was out of sight. He had been gone about 15 minutes around the side of the property and Sam felt uneasy.

Then, Sam gasped. She was aware she hadn't allowed herself to breath for a second or two and finally exhaling but covering her own mouth in fear of being heard, she let out a squeal.

Ahead of her, crossing the tree lined street, she could see a lady with a pushchair and small girl inside, but alongside her walked a small child resembling Grace and they were chatting and laughing as they left the house and crossing over to the park.

Sam looked to her left '*Where was Jed?*' She placed her hand on the door handle and initially opened the door, but something stopped her and she quietly pulled it too.

She took out her phone and tried to zoom in, taking a couple of pictures before dropping it onto Jed's empty seat.

This was possibly a Nanny seeing to the children? She was quite young, maybe 30s and it was warming to see how tender she was with the girls. Sam smiled, her breathing calmer, her heart pounding, terrified of doing the wrong thing.

She so wanted to call Mia, call the Police, then call everyone … *Joe was dead*? Her heart sank; Gracie loved her daddy. No, he was dead … he had been desperate, losing his wife, his business. We are human; we make mistakes and Sam knew Joe had spent the last 6 months of his life trying to correct his.

Jed ran across the road and hopped in the car.

'There are swings and girls' toys in the back garden' he began, excitedly. *'There is definitely more than one girl here, I saw coats, wellie boots and all sorts of pink toys in a playroom around the back. Sam, I think this is it ...* 'Jed then stopped, a wry smile appeared on his face. *'What*?' he asked.

Sam slowly pointed ahead and Jed's eyes followed.

'No!' he gasped, leaning on the steering wheel to get a better look.

'It's Grace' Sam oozed. *'That's our girl, 100% that's Grace'*

Jed flashed a look at Sam, then back at the group playing ahead.

'Let's go' he laughed, but Sam grabbed his arm and her desperate plea caused him to stop.

'It's ok Sam' he said, *'It will be ok'*

Sam shook her head *'No, this could be terrifying for her. It's been 6 months Jed. 6 months for her is a life-time, she may not recognise me and ...* 'Jed held her hand.

'We cannot lose her now Sam' he pleaded with her to trust him.

Sam knew that but then explained the need to do this bit right and of course she would intervene if they were to leave the park.

'*Call Jamie … now!*' she ordered. '*They can call it in to the Police. I'm calling Mia*'.

Waiting for Jamie gave Sam even more time to watch Grace at play and the months just fell away. She had changed, of course, but her curls, her smile and her little chubby body was just starting to stretch out a little. She was a little more agile and capable. It was utter joy. She had been loved and looked after … how could they have been so lucky? Lucky? What a thought? But in their experience 'lucky' was rarely the case.

Jed met Jamie further along the road and Sam stayed in the car to keep watch. It was the hardest thing she would be asked to do, to leave the scene and head to the Station without Gracie. But right now, she did not want to make any mistakes and Jamie would stay in her place.

She knew Mia needed to be collected and prepared and it was time to reunite her family.

Jamie even hugged Sam, praising her for perseverance and stamina to see it through, '*never wavering*' he praised.

By the time Mia and Sam arrived at the Station, little Gracie was in a side room playing with a child therapist, alongside her new little sister. Sam hoped so much that this little girl would prove to be Jose's and that they could reunite them.

There was no denying she had a better start in life than the one she would have had if she had been left with Jose and Rick, but now he was gone, Jose could have the opportunity to do better; but then Sam found herself wondering whether the child would have had a more hopeful future if she had been left undiscovered? ... *but that wasn't helping the situation now.*

The following hours were lengthy; exhausting, frustrating as everyone was desperate to get Grace home but these things take real time.

Mia was asked to identify her daughter and Sam bawled like a baby when she watched through the glass at Mia trying to talk to her; there was something in Gracie's eyes that recognised Mia, she even came over and shared a couple of toys with her. There was great hope, real possibility of this ending in a way Sam could only pray for.

Even though Mia struggled to leave the room when first asked, she flung her arms around Sam, thanking her and crying, squeezing the love out of her, sobbing with joy.

The door opened and Jamie popped his head round, acknowledging Mia with a smile, then gesturing at Sam that he needed to speak to her privately.

Sam kissed Mia's face and told her to wait, to carry on enjoying Grace and that she would be back as soon as she could.

When Sam re-entered the room, Mia was talking with two female officers and desperately trying to recall dates and times, then shaking her head in frustration as this took her attention away from her daughter. Finally, on Sam's request, they agreed to talk with Mia later and left the room. Once again, a grateful Mia hugged Sam tight.

'I knew you would find her' she cried. *'I just knew you would, but Mum, what have you been through?'* Mia looked down at her clothes and for the first time Sam realised she too was covered in blood and stank of beer.

'Oh, blimey' Sam giggled. *'Err, yes, that's ... um ... '.* Then she looked up and smiled at her daughter who was positively glowing.

They were disturbed once more when the door tapped and a fresh-faced officer entered the room. He asked if he could speak with Sam for a moment, so again Sam apologised to Mia and rose to leave the room. But as the door was closing, the officer was overheard saying they needed to talk about Joe and with that Mia joined them.

'What about Joe?' she asked, then with a panic in her voice added. *'Mum! We need to call Joe!'*

Sam stood in the doorway and she took a precious

moment to glance over at Gracie innocently playing and giggling, then back to Mia who waited for
guidance.

'*We still need to talk*' she sighed. '*... and soon,
I promise. There is so much to say*'.

This time Mia was beaming. '*No rush Mum, it can
wait.*'

Synopsis

The main characters, Sam & Jed, make up part of a team from the UK Missing Persons Bureau in London. They work directly with both UK and International Police and together they build patterns and share information, in hope of reuniting people.

Sam finds herself ultimately tested when Grace, her 2yr old granddaughter, goes missing and she soon realises, even with her years of experience and the Bureau's full co-operation, there are no shortcuts or guarantees.

People go missing every day; but the turmoil of not knowing, is the cruellest. So, when Sam is faced with such horror, the pressure is on to do what she does best; though taking her emotions out of the situation nearly leads to her downfall.

Her journey to get to the truth leads her to the unthinkable, to a place so dark, no child should ever know and if the price for answers is a deal with the devil himself, then that's a price she is willing to pay.

Jed is ex-force and his approach is to act fast; something Sam has been able to manage for most of their career. But now is the time for action; following protocol had not found a solution these past 6 months.

Finding Grace is every parent's nightmare ... but it begs the question; how far would you go?

ACKNOWLEDGE-MENT

To my family and friends, who have
supported and encouraged me to follow
my dreams; I thank you sincerely.
To my husband for always believing in
me and to our beautiful Mum, who went
on ahead of us, 25 years ago x

BOOKS IN THIS SERIES

Missing Persons Bureau

Finding Grace is the first in the series and where we first meet Sam & Jed.

They make up an integral part of a Missing Persons Bureau in London, assisting the Police both here in the UK and internationally.

Sam finds herself in the terrifying position of her own granddaughter, 2 yr old Grace, going missing. Every parent's nightmare, but it begs the question: How far would you go?

One More

One More takes a closer look at Jed, who remains haunted by his past.

But the desperation to find one more risks not only Jed's life, but that of his family and Sam's actions endanger them all.

She fears they may not survive.

Price To Pay

Price to Pay shows that every action has a consequence, yet when faced with fear and a need to protect, we seldom have the luxury of time.
The need to act is imminent; living with it, is forever.

BOOKS BY THIS AUTHOR

Going Home

Have you ever wondered what it would be like to just up and go?

Even those who believe they have it all worked out, can come unstuck.

But someone told me, if it was meant for you, it wouldn't pass you by and in this story of re-evaluation, Sarah finds herself facing the ultimate life test.

Going Home is more than a book title; it's a feeling you have when you head for safety, for reassurance and love and Sarah could never have imagined the surprises that lay ahead.

Her future held more secrets than her past.

Printed in Great Britain
by Amazon

67107230R00129